Edward A. Grainger's CASH LARAMIE

BULLETS
for a
BALLOT

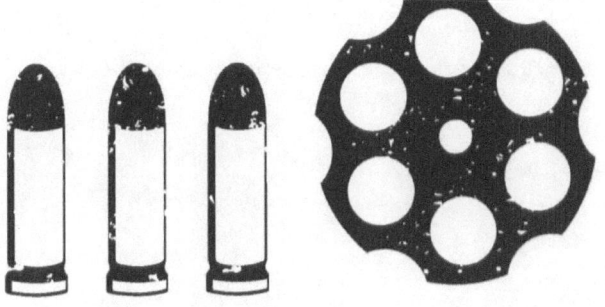

NIK MORTON

Cover images from Adobe Stock; cover design by dMix.

ISBN 978-1-943035-33-5

www.beattoapulp.com

Contents

Wouldn't You Like to Know

Wyoming, September, 1869

"The bitch is *dead*!" snarled Craig Bond as he wrestled with his saddle in Gillicuddy's Livery. He swore long and loud. "Women should know their place, Felix."

Cash backed away into the shadows. Neither Craig Bond nor Felix Penny had noticed him yet. Judging by their ungainly walk as they'd entered, they'd been hitting the bottle mighty hard. He'd seen the pair in action before—bullies. Big men who misused their superior weight and strength out of devil-driven anger.

"If Widow Traynor's dead, why're we saddling up to go to her place?" Felix asked, struggling with his own saddle as well as his dubious thought processes.

Craig let out a harsh laugh. "That's a manner of speaking, you idiot. I mean, she's as good as dead when we get there."

Cash heaved in a gulp of air but didn't make a sound. His Arapaho upbringing long since taught him when to remain silent and undetected. He glanced at the rear of the livery. The back door was open. Not ten minutes ago, he'd been out in the corral, putting Paint, his pinto, through his paces

1

before bringing him in for the night. He hunkered down and listened.

"Oh, I see," mumbled Felix, fiddling with his purple bandana. "You're too all-fired clever for me, Craig."

"Yeah, that's why I do all the planning, right?"

"You have a plan?"

"Yeah."

"What's the plan, Craig?"

Cash was eager to know as well. He absently fingered the arrowhead that hung from his neck.

"Dan and Hugo are waiting in the sheepherder's draw. Then us four are going to go calling on Widow Traynor. We'll burn her out. She's just too damned uppity, wanting women to vote. Next thing you know, women'll want to be mayor—even the President."

"That's right," Felix agreed. "Too uppity!"

"Yeah, well, I reckon all of us'll give her a poke before we silence her for good."

Cash swallowed hard and soundlessly backed away to the rear door. He'd heard enough. His first instinct was to rush round to Judge Hickey's place and report what he'd learned. But those other two, Dan and Hugo—whoever they were— were already on the trail. It would take time to tell the judge, and then they'd have to rouse Sheriff Adams and it would all take a lot of jawing. Talk was cheap. Time could cost Mrs. Traynor her life. Even at his age, he knew life was cheap too. But she was a nice lady, too young to be a widow, folk said. Attractive to boot—for an older woman of some twenty-one years, he reckoned. Sad and attractive, he thought, as he slid out the door and hurried over to the pinto.

* * *

The summer night-sky was clear, without blemish, pinpricked with stars. A glow approached from the east, but it wasn't the sunrise; paradoxically, it was something akin to darkness, the darkness of evil. Riding slightly ahead, Craig Bond led the other three men on toward Rancho Traynor, and he felt real good, their flaming torches glinting, throwing shadows over their faces.

"Hey, Widow!" he yelled, "You've got five minutes to get the hell out, or we burn you out!"

Beside him, Dan Fleming whooped.

Abruptly, a gun-flash briefly lit up the left-hand window of the ranch house and a shot barked.

Craig's horse reared in fright, and he dropped the torch.

Behind him, Hugo Letch laughed. "Widow's got you spooked, Craig."

Swirling round on his mount and putting the reins in his mouth, Craig pulled out his six-gun and fanned the weapon, firing blindly at the building. He grunted in satisfaction as he heard the glass of windows shattering.

"Felix, Hugo, torch the barn," Craig snarled, and quickly dismounted, leaving the horse ground-hitched.

He rushed to his left and ducked behind the water trough just in time. Bullets spat into the water, soaking his face and shoulders. "Damned bitch is gonna pay for this."

Dan landed alongside him, breathless.

Hugo and Felix rode toward the barn when, suddenly, a shotgun blasted at them from the loft. The buckshot spattered on the dirt in front of them.

"She's got help, damn her eyes," shouted Hugo.

Hurriedly dismounting, the pair rushed to the barn, brandishing their torches.

A shot rang out from the house. Felix let out a high-pitched shriek and buckled to the ground, a dark patch discoloring his pants leg. "I've been shot!" he yelled, leaning on an elbow. "Help me, Hugo!"

Hesitating, halfway to the barn door, Hugo said, "I'll come back when I've got that bastard." He gestured at the barn with his gun and fired two rapid shots at the loft when, alarmingly, another shot from the house sounded and his arm jerked. Blood spouted from his wrist and he dropped the weapon. "Shit, she got me!"

"With me, Dan," called Craig, ducking and running in a crouch as he moved to the rear of the barn.

* * *

His mouth dry and his heart pounding, Cash used his left hand to wipe blood from the scratch on his cheek, caused by splinters from a post gouged by Hugo's bullet.

He watched from the loft. The two called Hugo and Felix shouldn't trouble Mrs. Traynor anymore, he reckoned. They were out of it. He felt a tremor in his right hand. Sure, he'd shot at men before; it wasn't so long back when he'd shot dead those two owlhoots who terrorized Mrs. Hickey. That wasn't the same as now; that was a spur of the moment thing. From this vantage point, it was different, more cold-blooded, a bit like hunting antelope, he reckoned. He touched his bloody cheek. Only the antelope didn't shoot back. The two quite recent wounds in his thigh and shoulder tingled, as if reminding him of that sober fact.

Boots scuffed on the ground by the barn's back door.

Cash hefted the Greener he'd brought from the livery and soundlessly moved into the shadows of the loft, behind large bales of hay. Mrs. Traynor must be using that new hay baling machine that new farmer's group called the Grange had bought. Hanging on a hook nearby was an old, discarded workhorse harness.

"I don't know who the hell you are, but you're about to end up roasted meat!" Cash recognized the voice: Craig Bond.

A man's laughter erupted from the front entrance. "I like it, roast meat!" This must be Dan Fleming, Cash guessed. "Felix was right, you have a way with words."

"Yeah, well, let's torch this place and cook the trigger-happy son of a bitch."

"Okay, keep your shirt on," barked Dan. Cash heard him move close to the loft ladder, just underneath him.

At that moment, there was a rapid exchange of gunfire outside, and Dan's attention was drawn to the entrance.

With an almighty heave, Cash shouldered the bale of hay over the edge. In the dim light, he glimpsed Dan jerk his head round and stare up at the sound of the toppling bale. Too late, he raised a protective arm and fell beneath the hay.

In almost the same instant, Cash grabbed the heavy workhorse harness and jumped.

Taken completely unaware, Craig fired up into the loft by the ladder, but Cash was already in mid-air, his arms extended.

By luck or uncanny judgment, Cash dropped the harness over Craig's head and pinned the drunken man's arms to his side.

Cash's feet hit the hard-packed earth and he let go and rolled away.

Craig staggered, his gun still in his hand but pointed harmlessly at the ground. He swore and shook himself left and right in frustration, but he couldn't break free of the harness.

Cash snatched a pitchfork and jabbed the tines at Craig's feet, impaling them.

With a deafening scream, Craig tumbled over onto his back and let out another bellow as the harness pressed into his spine. "You bastard," he wheezed, "I'll get you for this."

"Maybe you will, Mr. Bond," Cash said, "but it ain't gonna be today."

"Seems to me, I needn't have hurried," Mrs. Traynor said at the doorway. "You've got everything in hand, young man." She lowered her Yellow Boy rifle, removed a slim cigar from her mouth, and lit a lantern hanging on a stall post.

"I was lucky, I guess," Cash said and shrugged as the light increased.

"What the hell," Craig growled, "he's only a kid!"

Mrs. Traynor walked past Craig, gave him a hefty kick with her boot and held out a cigar for Cash. "More of a man than you'll ever be," she told Craig.

She lit Cash's cigar.

He inhaled and started coughing.

"You don't smoke them like cigarettes," she said and chuckled.

Tears filled his eyes and he heard Craig laughing.

Cash walked over to Craig and hunkered down beside him. He blew on the tip of the cigar and held the red end about an inch from Craig's dark brown eyes. "You were planning on burning her out, right?"

Blinking furiously, sweat beading his brow, Craig croaked, "Yeah, but it was only for fun. We don't hold with women gettin' the vote, that's all. You're a man, you 'preciate that, don't you?"

The smell of singed hair and flesh flushed Cash's nostrils as he burned part of Craig's left eyebrow and the skin above it. "No, I don't appreciate it at all." He squashed the uncommon pleasurable feeling that threatened to swamp him and removed the cigar. He stood up and looked down at a surprisingly sober Craig Bond.

Tears trailed from the corners of Craig's eyes. "If I wasn't in this goddamned harness, you bastard, I'd whup you good."

"Wouldn't you like to think so?" Mrs. Traynor said and laughed. She turned on her heel. "Come on, young man, let's get this sorry lot back to Cheyenne. Mind you, jail's too good for at least one of them."

As he emerged from the barn, Cash understood what she meant. "That one's Hugo Letch," she said, pointing her rifle at the man sprawled on the ground, bloody and dead.

"He didn't want to put down his weapon," she added, "so I had no choice, I put him down."

The smell of death wasn't unusual. Cash had grown up with it. But somehow this was different. This death seemed right, appropriate.

It took them the better part of half an hour to get ready. Cash hitched the buckboard team and helped Mrs. Traynor heave the corpse of Hugo onto the man's horse. Still secured by the harness, Craig was shoved onto the flatbed, alongside the unconscious Dan Fleming and the wounded Felix Penny.

* * *

"This is a sorry mess," said Judge Evan J. Hickey as Sheriff Adams locked the jailhouse. He'd put the three captives in separate cells. He shook his head, his slicked back thinning brown hair sprinkled with gray. "Tempers are a mite flared up, I warrant, over this women's vote business."

"It will happen," Mrs. Traynor said. "Sooner or later. It's about time people accept it." She laughed. "I shouldn't wonder if many a wife might withhold her tenderness unless her spouse lets the bill pass."

"That may be the case, Mrs. Traynor." His brown eyes sparkled. "I suspect Mrs. Julia Bright has a hand in it."

"Probably. Anyway, Mr. Bright's bill is clear enough. Every woman twenty-one years or older, residing in this Territory, may at every election to be held under the law thereof, cast her vote."

"I know the arguments, Ma'am, and I tend to agree with them," the judge stated. "Suffrage should be a basic right of American citizenship."

"Amen to that," she said.

The judge fingered his strong squared chin and turned to Cash. "I reckon you've proved yourself yet again, son." He put a hand on Cash's shoulder. "I want you to stay out at Mrs. Traynor's place until the votes are cast. Will you do that for me?"

Cash glanced at Mrs. Traynor.

She nodded and smiled at him. "If you hadn't rode in and warned me," she said, "well, things might have turned out real different."

* * *

Cash woke when the night's blanket still covered the land. Through the bare window, stars that had witnessed the attack and a bloody death shone just as before, as if nothing of great importance had happened. The moon was full and tinted everywhere inside with a blue shade.

He sat up on the bearskin bed he'd made across the doorway.

Mrs. Traynor paced the other end of the room, sometimes gazing out the window. Moonglow revealed her limbs under the white cotton nightdress. Cash looked down—his long johns had been white, once, he reckoned, but a long time ago, before he acquired them. There was a vaguely familiar stirring in his loins and he self-consciously pressed it away. He peered up but she hadn't noticed.

Then she turned to face him, running her hands over her upper arms.

"Are you cold?" He was warm, surprisingly flushed.

"No, just chilled by memories."

Sure that his long johns no longer presented an embarrassment, he stood and snagged a blanket off the back of a chair. He moved over to her. "Here," he said and wrapped it around her shoulders.

"Thank you for tonight." Her eyes were dark, and her hair was raven black. A musky scent rose from her as she adjusted the blanket.

"Glad I got here in time, Mrs. Traynor." He turned to move back to his bearskin bed.

She reached out and grasped his hand. "Esther. Call me Esther."

He nodded. "Sure, Esther."

She smiled and let out a small sigh. "Since my husband passed, no man has called me that."

"It's a fine name, Esther. Comes from the Bible, doesn't it?"

Esther chuckled. "You're full of surprises, young man. Yes, it does."

He moved a foot and glanced down. Something was amiss all right. "I'd better get back to …" He half-turned to the bearskin on the floor.

"Don't go," she whispered, her breath fanning his cut cheek. He could still feel her fingers, gently bathing the small cut, and smell her nearness, a mixture of lavender and bakery—flour and cinnamon. His stomach rumbled at the thought of food.

"Seems to me you're hungry for something," she observed.

He nodded, his mouth dry. As dry as when he'd fired at Hugo and Felix. But this was different. His stomach somersaulted and his flesh tingled in anticipation. "When you said to the judge about wives withholding tenderness, I knew what you meant," he said, and he felt his cheeks grow warm. "But I've never been …"

Gently, she placed a warm finger over his lips. "I know, I know." With the same hand, she brushed a tendril of hair from his brow. "The first time can be precious," she said, "so it has to be your decision." She cupped his face in her hands. "You must say. Do you want this?"

"Yes," he said, though he reckoned it came out as a croak. "I want …"

"Then, even though I shouldn't be doing this, I reckon I must abide by my young savior's wishes." Gently, she took his hand and led him to her bedroom.

* * *

He lay on his side as dawn light streamed through the glass window. At least this one hadn't been shot out. He didn't seem able to explain how he felt. It was wonderful, as if his heart and mind soared, an experience unlike anything he'd ever known. His warm skin tingled as he recalled how Esther kissed his young body's scars and let her tears fall on them.

She had pointed to the unusual scars on his back, on both sides.

"I got these when I did the sun dance," he told her proudly.

"When you were with the Arapaho?"

"Yes. I had to dance while dragging a buffalo skull that's hitched to my flesh."

She shuddered. "That's awful."

"No, it's quite normal. We learned early to shut out pain."

She hugged him then.

Esther was warm, considerate and loving. Very loving. He learned so much from her under the moonlight and wondered when he'd finally fallen asleep.

Now he watched her as she sat naked at an ornate mahogany dressing table. Her raven hair hung down her strong muscular back and she idly brushed it. He caught her reflection in the flyblown mirror. "You look serious," he said.

"I was just thinking that you'll make some woman a good husband. You're a fast learner and an attentive lover."

He grinned, his chest swelling. "Really?"

She laughed. "Really—and don't get too cocky about it!"

Then they both laughed as they realized what she'd said.

He swung his legs out of bed. "Can we do it again, Esther?"

She pivoted on her stool and eyed him. "You mean four times in one night isn't enough?"

"It isn't night any more."

"So it isn't." She stood and drifted toward him.

* * *

Afterward, he puffed on one of her cheroots and said, "You know, I could get to like this."

"What, the cigar?"

He grinned and blew out blue smoke. "Yes, that too."

She chuckled. "You scamp, you!"

He leveled his eyes on hers and his tone turned serious. "I want to marry you, Esther. I love you."

"Wouldn't you like to think so?"

"I do."

She shook her head. "No, you don't. You love the feeling I give you."

He moved his head to and fro in protest. "No, that's not it."

"Sure, you like me."

"But … you need a man in your life. Someone to love you and care for you."

Moisture brimmed her eyes. "I honestly don't think you're the marrying kind, young man. I suspect you've got the wanderlust in you." She sighed. "I've seen it in men before."

Cash nodded. "Judge Hickey says I got that from my parents."

Esther smiled. "The judge and his wife are real fond of you, aren't they?"

"Yes, they've been good to me. They knew my parents … before they came west." He smiled. "You've been good to me, too."

"You can't go falling in love with everybody who's good to you. No more than you can go killing those who're bad to you." She shook her head. "No, son, marriage isn't possible. Besides, there's quite an age difference—maybe six or seven years. If the judge knew what we've been up to, he'd likely sentence me to hard labor for corrupting a minor."

"I did my Sun Dance just before I left the tribe and met the judge," he said earnestly. "I'm fully grown …"

She glanced down. "You sure are, son." She flicked the sheet over him, forming a little tent. "But that's enough for now. Remember, you're supposed to be guarding my ranch and me. What if the sheriff or the judge rode out to see how we were set?"

He chuckled. "I reckon they'd be mighty jealous."

Laughing, she swatted him with a pillow.

* * *

The trial was held at the end of that week and the courthouse was packed. Cash sat on a bench beside Martha Hickey, a smart woman of about fifty who seemed several years younger when she gazed on her husband, the judge. In front of them sat the prosecuting attorney, Mr. Grist who had an annoying habit of using the phrase "It's all grist to the mill." He was certainly known to grind down the opposition with complex arguments and relentless persistence. Still, Cash thought his joke was wearing a bit thin.

The defense, Mr. Nash, sitting beside the three accused men, argued for leniency, considering the three men were drunk.

"I like a tipple the same as the next man," countered Mr. Grist, his sideburns bristling. "But threatening to burn a widow out of hearth and home is no drunken prank."

Abruptly, Craig Bond stood up. "It was just a bit of fun," he snapped. "It's getting' that women don't know their place."

A few men grumbled in agreement, while all the women—at least half those present—vociferously berated the men. Cash suspected that a few women might be withholding their tenderness tonight.

"Silence in my court!" barked the judge and slammed down his gavel.

As quiet descended, Judge Hickey said, "This is not a political meeting but a court of law. You three men blatantly breached the law. I don't need a jury to tell me different, but I must ask the jury foreman all the same." He leveled his stare at the hapless thin man at the end of the jury bench. "Well?"

"Y-your honor, we find Craig Bond and Felix Penny guilty as charged."

The judge pointed his gavel at the third man, Dan Fleming, who sat throughout the proceedings staring vacantly into space. "And what about this man?"

"We think he's probably guilty, judge, but considering the state of his mind, we ain't sure what to declare."

Judge Hickey let out an exasperated sound. "Very well. Guilty, he is!" He slammed down the gavel. Eyeing each accused man in turn, he said, "I don't hold with violence of any kind in or around Cheyenne. I stamp down on the perpetrators *hard*. You men are no exception. You're all sentenced to twenty years imprisonment."

His pronouncement was accompanied by a few gasps, doubtless from the relatives of the sentenced men.

A handful of women cheered.

"Silence in the court!" shouted the bailiff.

When silence was restored, the bailiff announced, "All rise for the judge."

Judge Hickey stood and stormed out of the room.

* * *

Once the three men were taken away to serve their sentence, Cheyenne returned to normal. Cash felt a little guilty, staying with Esther when there was no longer any threat. But only a little guilty. In all other ways, he loved every moment.

He worked on her ranch, learning new skills. From time to time, he returned to Cheyenne and helped at the livery, but his heart was no longer in it and Bowler Gillicuddy sensed his change. "You've been a darned good worker and a big help to me, Cash," Bowler said. "But I reckon you need to spread your wings more. Go on, git—and don't worry none about me, I'll get somebody else to give me a hand—though I doubt if I'll be as lucky again."

Cash rushed into Esther's ranch house, grinning. "Bowler's let me go!"

She stood at the table, her face patterned with white flour as she kneaded dough. "That means you'll be under my feet all day, I reckon."

"I was thinking of being under more than your feet, Esther."

She laughed. "You're incorrigible, Cash Laramie, you really are!" She sighed. "Well, if Bowler has an idea about us, I imagine a few other townspeople have guessed by now."

"Is it so wrong?"

"Right and wrong aren't always black and white, young man. I'd have thought you'd learned that by now."

"Well, yes, I suppose I have." He kissed her cheek. "And I know that this is right."

He still regularly visited the Hickeys and they kept him up with the politics and gossip of the region, though little mention was made of Mrs. Traynor. Surprisingly, Mrs. Hickey seemed pleased for him. Yet, whenever Mrs. Traynor was mentioned, the judge's face turned a light puce color.

Cash thrived on hard work and outdoor activities.

As the months passed by, his muscles developed due to the manual labor and good food. And plenty of loving.

Cash forgot all about Craig Bond, Felix Penny and Dan Fleming. He had fields to plow, fences to fix and meat to bring to the dinner table.

Although there was no campaign, public display or debate regarding the female suffrage, the twenty member Territorial Legislature approved the revolutionary measure. Perhaps the decision had something to do with the number of women who kept vigil outside Governor John A. Campbell's office. Whatever the impetus, he signed the bill into law on December 10, 1869.

"That's it, Cash," Esther said. "You can't stay here anymore."

"Why?"

"You have no legitimate reason. No varmints can change the law by bothering me—or any other woman, come to that." She beamed at him. "We've won!"

He was overjoyed for her, but saddened too.

"Don't linger in Cheyenne," she advised. "Go out and live your life. Then return when you feel ready."

She winked and handed him her Yellow Boy rifle. "Take this, you might need it. And you know, I suspect the judge has plans for your future."

CHAPTER 1

Desecration

Wyoming, July, 1885

"You wanted to see me?" Cash said as he entered Chief U.S. Marshal Devon Penn's office, an unlit cigar dangling from his mouth. Begrudgingly, he respected his boss's persistent emphasis on a smoke-free office. But he still liked the feel of a cheroot between his teeth.

"Yes, I've got an interesting little job for you." Penn raised his large bulk from the desk at his large wooden desk and walked round to sit in one of two Windsor armchairs; he gestured at the other.

Cash removed his hat and then sank into the leather upholstery.

Penn said, "Heard of a town called Bear Pines? It's on Bear Creek."

"Can't say I have. I don't reckon I've been that way for a long while."

"Well, it makes no difference." He ran stubby fingers through his thinning mousy hair. "You're needed there."

"Needed? In what way, needed?"

"There's a battle brewing." Penn grinned, his hazel eyes amused.

Cash shifted in his seat. "In that case, I don't think you need me, you need the army."

Penn chuckled, his double chin wobbling slightly. "Oh, this is quite different, it's a battle between the sexes."

Puzzled now, Cash leaned forward. "I can see you're enjoying this. So, go on, enlighten me."

"Very well. There's a woman—a Mrs. Tolliver—running for the job of mayor."

"A woman mayor, eh? I haven't heard of one—though I know of a couple of female justices of the peace."

"Well, the citizens of Bear Pines are split down the middle. The sitting mayor, a guy named Brett Nolan, has powerful allies, it seems."

"Don't tell me, a few old chauvinists are against her, making threats?"

Penn shook his head. "If that was all, I'm sure Mrs. Tolliver could handle it. She sounds like a formidable woman." He wafted a two-page letter. "No, the threats aren't idle—it's turning a mite ugly, and the threats are liable to get lethal."

"So you want me to read the riot act, is that it?"

Penn nodded. "Something like that. The town's lucky enough to have a judge. Virgil McPiece. I've met him a couple of times. He's a good man."

"Aren't all judges?"

"I'll ignore that. Anyway, the election's at the end of the month, so it'll probably all settle down afterward."

* * *

"Settle down a spell," the sheriff said, rising from a rocking chair to one side of his office door. "Not often I get to chinwag with a U.S. Marshal."

Dismounting, Cash grinned. "Is that java I can smell?"

"Sure is. Always got some on the go." He went inside. "You're welcome, come on in."

Cash tethered Paint to the hitching rail. "Won't be long, fella, then I'll see to your needs."

The office was dark in contrast to the brightness of the street. Cash pulled off his black Stetson, hung it on the back of a chair. The pot-bellied stove was at the far side of the office. The sheriff poured the dark liquid into a tin mug. "Sugar?"

"Nope."

"Sheriff Clem Hain," he said, handing over the mug.

"Cash Laramie. Thanks." He sipped the hot liquid. "Yeah, I needed that."

"What're you doing here, Marshal? Far as I know, Bear Pines is peaceful and no owlhoots have ridden through for months."

"Your town's just on my route from here to there." He thumbed at the open doorway. "I see you've got an election for mayor."

"Yes, you can't miss the banners and posters, eh?"

"Who's the mayor?"

"Brett Nolan. He's done a lot for the town, so I'm sure he'll get re-elected."

Cash sipped his coffee. "Glad to hear it." He strode over to the window, gazed out. "Judging by the amount of bunting and advertisements, I'd reckon the mayor's taking no chances. Seems like he has someone to contest him, is that right?"

Sheriff Hain laughed. "Nobody of any account. It's a woman, in fact." He shook his head. "Would you believe it? A darned woman as mayor? No, it ain't ever going to happen."

Smiling, Cash lowered the mug. "Would that be a Mrs. Tolliver?"

The sheriff's face hardened instantly. "You've heard about her?" he said, his tone deeply questioning.

"Just rumor."

Hain shrugged. "Well, that's all she can manage in her sorry campaign. Silly rumors."

Snagging his hat, Cash said, "Thanks for the java, Sheriff." They shook hands. "I need a bath, a shave, a good meal—but before that, I want to get my horse seen to."

Hain escorted him to the door and pointed to the right, down the street. "Old Frank at Ferguson's Livery will do your horse proud, Marshal. Can't miss it—two blocks past the Thorndike Hotel."

* * *

After he'd left his pinto in the care of Frank Ferguson, Cash made his way to the imposing two-story mansion at the far end of town. The shingle said, *Judge Virgil McPiece.* As he mounted the portico steps, he hoped his honor was as straightforward and uncompromising as his sign.

Judge Virgil McPiece answered the door. His flowing white hair reached down to his shoulders, eyebrows thick and unruly. His gray eyes sparkled.

Cash introduced himself.

"Marshal Laramie, good to see you," the judge said, his tone subdued but sociable. He held out his hand. "Come in for a drink, won't you?" He ushered Cash into the hall.

"A quick one, Judge, if that's okay with you. I just wanted to let you know I'm in town. Right now, all I want is a decent meal, a bath and some shuteye."

"Very well." He gestured at the staircase at the end of the hall. "My wife Lisa's an invalid upstairs—that's why my welcome mightn't seem too warm."

"Sorry to hear that, your honor. You sure I'm not disturbing you both?"

"No, no—let's retire to my study."

As they sat with their tumblers of whiskey, the judge outlined the opposition to Mrs. Tolliver. "Mayor Brett Nolan has spent some time buying up land and people. Nolan's staunchest follower is a rancher called Lance Jacobson. He's got two sons who do as he tells them."

Cash sipped the whiskey; it was quality stuff, like nectar to his dry throat. "Sheriff Hain seems against Mrs. Tolliver."

The judge nodded his white head. "Oh, he is. He does what the mayor says. Though from time to time I can persuade him to apply the law even-handed." He laughed, a barking sound of derision. "But only when it doesn't interfere with his patron's business, of course."

"A pity. Other than his intolerance of Mrs. Tolliver, he seemed okay."

"Most folk are—until Nolan gets his claws into them. Sucks the goodness out of them, I reckon!" He stroked his chin. "Our esteemed bank manager is currently sitting on the political fence. Nolan's been working on him for months, but still Martin Plampin hasn't committed to either Mayor Nolan or Mrs. Tolliver."

"But if Nolan sends plenty of business Plampin's way, he might fold?"

"Undoubtedly. Plampin exists to make money and more money."

"Anyone else of note?"

"No, not really. The men I've mentioned are influential. What they say and do affects others. I'd say almost all the men of the town are happy to stick with Nolan—the devil they know ... Even the shopkeepers who have reason to vote out the sheriff and Nolan don't want to openly antagonize the mayor—"

"Seems to me you've got a town ruled by fear and intimidation."

The judge nodded. "But don't get me wrong. They're mostly good people. Just need a little decent leadership. I speak out when I can—choosing my battles with care."

"Have you had any threats, Judge?"

He pursed his lips. "Only the usual. Disgruntled miscreants reluctant to pay their fines, that sort of thing. Nothing too serious, though. Why?"

"The letter Mrs. Tolliver sent to my boss at the federal building, talks about threats to her life."

"I didn't know that. Devon simply sent me a wire telling me you were coming."

Cash stood and shook hands with the judge. "Thanks for that, anyway, sir. I reckon my stomach can't hold off any longer, it needs a solid meal."

"There are two hotels—go for the Wordsworth, the sheets are cleaner and the bedbugs aren't as hungry."

"Thanks, Judge." They moved to the door and Judge McPiece opened it.

The judge clapped a hand on Cash's shoulder. "Drop by again when you're able. I want to hear about that rapscallion Penn!"

Rapscallion? He can't be talking about the same man, surely? Yet they were much the same age. Cash shrugged. "It's a date, Judge." He tipped his hat and stepped down.

* * *

Early next morning, Cash set out on Paint, following the directions in Mrs. Tolliver's letter.

As he crested a rise, he reined in. Below, down a gentle slope of meadow grass was the Double-Bar T ranch. It was a pleasing sight, a single-story ranch house in the middle of a fenced acre; two outbuildings at the back; a barn and a small bunkhouse; and a corral—all within the fenced enclosure. Two horses were hitched at a rail at the front porch. Maybe Mrs. Tolliver had visitors. Also at the rear of the house was a vegetable garden, a stand of lodgepole pines and a grave headstone. Beyond the fence, meadows sloped in every direction, until they reached encircling conifers.

Cash squinted, certain he detected movement at the side of the house. People—four of them—a woman and three men, he reckoned, walking toward the grave. Without moving his gaze from those figures, he reached behind and pulled his spyglass from the left-hand saddlebag. Extending the metal tube, he brought the people close up. The woman wore a gingham dress and it was torn at the front. Her gray-streaked black hair fell in disarray over her face. One man was a boy, about fifteen, he supposed, and the other two men held guns, threatening the woman and the boy, with big grins on their faces.

It looked like the threats Mrs. Tolliver suffered were about to turn lethal.

Damn. Cash rammed shut the spyglass, shoved it in the saddlebag. "Let's git, Paint!" He rode hard down the slope, his course slanted toward the back of the ranch house.

Damn, he doubted he'd be in time. Halfway down the slope, Cash reined in and pulled out his rather worn Yellow Boy Winchester rifle.

"Steady, boy," he whispered, taking aim.

Paint snorted and obediently stood still.

* * *

Mrs. Tolliver stumbled toward a stand of three lodgepole pine trees that cast their shadow over her husband Dean's grave. People with good intentions had told her the grave was too close to the house, but she insisted. Dean often sat under the trees, reading. Now, her bedroom window overlooked his last resting place. Halfway there, ignoring the pistol barrel digging in her back, she stopped and turned. She glanced fearfully at her fifteen-year-old son, Danny. His dark hair swept across his face; a bruise had formed on his cheek. He gripped the spade handle tightly, his knuckles white. Towering over him was an enormous man named Tiny. He was the opposite of his name, over six feet tall, and very broad. Huge, not with muscle, but with plenty of fat. He reeked of body odor and other smells.

Her heart hammered in her chest and her hands felt its pounding as she attempted to hold together the torn dress fabric. "Please, leave us alone! I'll step down—give the mayor his victory."

"You hear that, Tiny?" The speaker had called himself as Ash when the two men rode up while Danny was splitting wood. The chopping block was just on his left, near the clapboard wall of the house, the axe embedded with its handle sticking out at an angle. She'd stood outside the door as the men approached. The surly pair drew their weapons before she could reach for her Winchester that leaned against the wall just inside the doorway.

Now, under the guns of Ash and Tiny, Danny slowly thrust the spade into the loamy earth.

Ash laughed. "She wants to step down."

Danny stopped, his vibrant blue eyes appealing to her, anxious.

"Yeah, Ash, mighty obligin' of her, considerin' ..." Tiny slammed the butt of his rifle into Danny's back, nearly sending him to his knees. "Keep diggin', boy!"

With an effort, she fought down her last meal. She wouldn't amuse them by being sick. Though she was sick at heart and winced as Danny stoically recovered from the blow and continued to dig a shallow grave.

"I'm feeling generous. Your brat can dig a grave just for one," growled Ash. "Close to your husband."

"One?" she queried.

"Yeah, and you get to choose who goes in it." He laughed but his narrow eyes never left hers. "You or your son."

She gripped her torn dress tight in her fist, a fist she'd willingly pound into that bastard Ash's face, if he lowered his six-gun even for an instant. Rage roiled in her gut, battling with knee-weakening fear.

"I like that," Tiny said.

Ash grinned, thrusting the barrel of his revolver against Mrs. Tolliver's cheek. "You'll like this more, friend."

"What's that?"

"If she enjoys it while we poke her, we might even let them both live!"

She bit her lip as Danny stopped digging and furtively eyed the axe. He hadn't a chance against guns; she hastily shook her head and her son leaned on the spade, his face scrunched up with concern for her.

"You don't mean that," she said. "You won't let us go, not now."

"You mean," Tiny said, "I get to poke 'er as well?"

"Sure. After me." Ash looked at her with malevolence in his eyes, and then winked.

A chill ran through her. These men were beyond evil.

Tiny grinned, showing brown tombstones of teeth. "Sure, that's okay. After you." He slapped at Danny's ear with his free hand. "Who said you could stop diggin'?"

Danny resumed digging, and Ash thrust Mrs. Tolliver down on the ground, on top of her husband's grave.

Her head smacked against the headstone, which was inscribed *Dean Tolliver, Born April 2, 1835 - Died May 31, 1885. Beloved father and son.* Unfortunately, she wasn't knocked out, though the blow hurt like Hades.

Slightly dazed, she looked up and wished she hadn't.

Ash growled, "Let the kid watch, Tiny. We're going to enjoy this." With one hand he leveled the revolver on her while with the other he unbuckled his belt and his pants dropped. He leered. "Lift your skirts, bitch."

"No! Please, no!" She hated herself as she begged.

"Yes—or your son fills the grave he's dug next to his pappy's right now." He half turned and aimed the six-gun at Danny.

Her heart was breaking as she lay on her husband's grave. Now the swine wanted to desecrate Dean's final resting place. She bit her lip. She must save Danny, if she could. That was uppermost in her mind as she reluctantly raised her dress.

Suddenly, Ash sank to his knees between her legs. "Yes, this is going to be fun." He laughed, his mouth wide.

Then blood gushed from his mouth, together with bits of bone and flesh and teeth, splattering her face and clothes. In the same instant, a rifle shot echoed round the valley and Ash bit the dirt that covered her husband. Appalled, she tugged her legs out from under him.

Trembling, fearful for her son, she rose to her knees.

Danny swung the spade at Tiny's head, but it had little effect—perhaps his brains weren't located there. But that move bought the lad a couple of seconds, long enough for him to dive away from the grave toward the chopping block. He grabbed the axe and swung it round. The axe-head sank into Tiny's vast belly.

Tiny growled, "You're dead, boy. Squashed like a bug!" His eyes glared, almost starting from his head and his face turned purple with rage.

She struggled to her feet, ready to rush to Danny's aid.

Then one of Tiny's glaring eyes changed color. It sprouted blood and brains and a gaping hole appeared in its place, while the echo of this second shot died. The enormous bulk of Tiny fell forward, into the shallow grave that wasn't big enough for him.

* * *

Cash shoved the rifle back in its scabbard and urged Paint on down the slope.

Finally, as his horse attained level ground at the fence, Cash eased Paint into a steady trot to the gate, where the shingle crossbar read *Double-Bar T*.

He rounded the ranch house corner.

Mrs. Tolliver stood in the shadow of the lodgepole pines, near the headstone of a grave, a Winchester in her arms, seemingly unmindful of the torn front of her dress. Her chest heaved and she was lathered in sweat. At her side was the young man, presumably her son; he seemed to wear his bruised face with some pride, and held a bloody axe warily. The whites of their eyes glinted, otherwise their features were indistinct.

He slowed Paint to a walk. "I mean you no harm, Mrs. Tolliver." He reined in and dismounted. He gave Paint a pat on the neck. "I'm a U.S. Marshal, here in response to your letter."

She stepped out of the shadow. "When I gave you my old gun, Cash Laramie, I never expected you to save my life with it!"

"Esther?"

CHAPTER 2

Gamble with Lives

"We've got a lot of catching up to do," she said. "This is Danny, my son."

"Pleased to meet you, Danny." Cash shook the boy's hand and nodded at the dead hulk. "You stood up well against that monster."

Danny brushed dark hair out of his eyes. "I didn't realize how fat he was—that axe should've done for him, but …"

"Never mind, son," Esther Tolliver said. "The marshal saw to him, all right."

"He did that!" Danny grinned, his blue eyes shining in admiration at Cash.

"First, however," Esther said, "I reckon we'd better get these sorry carcasses back to town before they stink more than they already do."

"Yeah, they could've done with a bath, I'd say."

"Well, now they can roast in hell."

Cash was surprised at the vehemence in her voice. Esther seemed harder now and he wondered what had changed her.

Maybe the death of her husband? He'd find out in time, he reckoned.

As he helped Danny load the two bodies onto the flat bed of the buckboard, Cash kept glancing at the young man, as if drawn by something familiar, yet he couldn't identify it. "Have we met before, Danny?" he finally asked.

"Possibly, sir—I often go into Bear Pines, buying stuff for Ma."

"I haven't been to Bear Pines before," Cash said, covering the bodies with a tarp from the barn.

Danny shrugged. "Well, in that case, we can't have met, Marshal. I haven't traveled much."

"Whereas," said Esther Tolliver, "from what I've heard, Cash Laramie, you've traveled a great deal."

Cash nodded. "I've been around. I guess I went out and lived my life."

"Glad to hear it," she said and climbed onto the driver's seat.

Danny tethered the horses of Tiny and Ash to the rear of the buckboard.

Danny and Cash rode on either side of the buckboard and they all headed toward town. Cash said, "What did those two say about the election?"

She frowned. "That's odd, I guess. They never once said anything about the election. I assumed that was why they came, of course. After those threatening letters, it seemed the next step."

"Ma ain't easily railroaded," Danny said with pride in his voice.

"I know, son," Cash said. "We met a long time back— before you were born. So I …"

He glanced at her, a question poised on his lips. He caught Esther looking at him and she smiled. "Wouldn't you like to know …" she said and left it at that.

No, it wasn't possible. She'd have gotten word to him. But he'd been only a youngster, certainly not capable of bringing up a family. Thoughts whirled around in his head.

"I met Dean a month or so after you left," she said, breaking the silence. "It was a whirlwind romance. He swept me off my feet. He was a lawyer and dabbled in politics."

"I'm pleased for you, Esther," Cash said, and meant it.

She smiled and her face lit up, briefly. "Before I knew it, I'd sold up and gone with him, campaigning in a few towns 'til we settled here, where Danny was born."

"When did your husband die?"

Her eyes narrowed. She slapped the horses with the reins, urging them to move faster. "About four weeks ago."

"How'd it happen?"

She was silent and he saw something glisten on her cheek.

"Sorry," he said, "I shouldn't bring it up, I guess."

"Pa was bushwhacked, Marshal," said Danny, bringing his mount alongside. "He'd thrown his hat in the ring to contest for mayor. Both me and Ma reckon the mayor paid for his murder in a dark alley, but we ain't got any proof."

"I was damned if Mayor Nolan was going to get his way!" Esther snapped, the back of a hand wiping her eyes. "I put myself forward in Dean's stead."

"That's either very brave or mighty foolish of you," Cash said.

"Foolish, I suspect." The reins slackened in her hands and the horses slowed. "I never counted on Danny being at risk.

But I should have." She let out a big sigh. "As soon as we've dumped these bodies, I'll go to the town hall and withdraw my name from the election."

"Ma, you can't do that!" Danny slammed a fist on his saddle horn. "I won't let you do that because of me."

Cash called across, "I'm here now, son. Maybe your ma won't have to give up."

Danny's blue eyes, slightly glazed with tears, gazed at him, trusting. "Really, Marshal?"

Cash eyed Esther and nodded. "Yes, I reckon Mayor Nolan can get licked without either your ma or you coming to grief."

Tears brimmed her eyes now. "I pray to God you're right, Cash." She turned back to the buckboard's horses. "Move it, damn you!"

* * *

"Damn me, Marshal, what've you got there?" Sheriff Hain said, rising from his rocker. As he walked to the edge of the boardwalk, he gave Esther a brief furtive glare.

"A couple of would-be murderers, Sheriff," Cash said, dismounting.

"Murderers, you say?" Hain took off his hat, scratched his head.

Peeling back the tarp from the bodies, Cash added, "Tiny and Ash. Recognize them?"

Sheriff Hain shook his head and wiped sweat from his brow. "No, can't say I do." He put his hat on again. "Damned hot, ain't it?"

"Yes, it is," Esther said. "That's why we brought them in—for burying before they get too ripe."

"Wait a damned minute. What about this murder business? What happened?"

"Those two men were seconds away from murdering Mrs. Tolliver and her son," Cash said. "If I hadn't come along, you'd be investigating a double killing."

"Well, in that case, thank you, Marshal, for saving me all that time and effort." He kicked the side of the buckboard. "Take them over to Rance Peel's," he said, thumbing at the funeral parlor two blocks down on the other side of the street. "He'll go through their pockets to see what kinda send-off they can afford."

"They were carrying $500 apiece," Cash said. "I've confiscated it." As the sheriff hesitated on a retort, Cash added, "I've filled in a receipt, and I'll leave it with the judge. Get your undertaker to bill me and Judge McPiece'll deduct it from the dead men's money."

"What about the rest of the money, Marshal?"

"That just might be evidence." He gestured at the corpses. "Neither man dressed as though he was worth five dollars, let alone five hundred. I reckon it was blood money for killing Mrs. Tolliver and her son."

Hain let out what seemed like an exaggerated gasp. "That's terrible. Who'd do such a thing, Marshal?"

"Wouldn't you like to know," Cash said, and swung Paint round toward the undertaker's. Esther and Danny had tied his horse to the buckboard and joined Esther on the driver's seat. They followed Cash without uttering another word.

By the time they got to Peel's Emporium for the Deceased, a sizeable crowd had gathered.

Peel opened the funeral parlor door and stood, wringing his hands expectantly, a tall, portly man with a florid complexion. He pointed at the two pairs of boots sticking out from the tarp. "New customers, I take it?" he said, his voice thin and irritating.

"Yes," Cash said, peeling back the tarp. "Two—though one of them'll probably take up two coffins by his lonesome."

Peel pursed his lips. "That'll be extra, taking into consideration the size of him."

"If I'm not around, send the bill to the judge. He'll settle with you."

"Very well." Peel gestured at his two black-clad assistants, and they hurried forward and hefted Ash onto a stretcher. They looked at Tiny and blanched. The crowd of onlookers melted away, several screwing up their faces at the odor that wafted toward them.

"The basic funeral, I take it?" Peel said.

"The cheapest," Cash said. "If you had a crematorium, I'd ask for that—seems to me that's where they're headed anyway, the flames of Hell."

"That's as maybe," said the undertaker, "but according to the good book, all men may be redeemed."

"The good book got it wrong where those two are concerned, Mr. Peel."

Once the two funeral assistants heaved Tiny away, their legs buckling, Esther said, "I've got to drop in on the printer, Marshal. See you there?"

Cash nodded.

She moved the horses off.

Cash wheeled his horse away and then had second thoughts. "Just a minute, Mr. Peel, I'll double your fee if you'll follow my wishes regarding these two miscreants."

"Sure, Marshal. What are your wishes."

Cash leaned down from his pinto and whispered in the undertaker's ear.

"My God," Peel seethed, backing away. "That's not done in this town. Maybe it happened in the old days in those dens of iniquity, but never here in Bear Pines."

Leaning on his pommel, Cash said, "Will you do it? Double fee, I said."

Showing reluctance that Cash knew was false, the undertaker finally nodded. "Very well. For two days, you say?"

"That's right. And afterward, bury them cheap and do it quick."

* * *

When Cash reached the printer's shop, he found Esther Tolliver standing on an empty wooden crate, addressing a gathering—mainly women—outside.

Her face flushed and her eyes alight with enthusiasm, she said, "I've just returned from my home with a U.S. Marshal, and we brought the dead bodies of two men who intended to murder me and my son." She gestured at Danny, who stood next to a young blonde girl in a pretty bonnet, a sheepish grin on his face.

The crowd murmured. But no one heckled, Cash noted.

"I ask you," Esther went on, "is it just coincidence or was there something more sinister behind their evil intentions?"

"It's shameful, the goings on lately in this town!" shouted a middle-aged woman.

"The law's only there for the big businesses," shouted a short store-holder, still in his apron. "The rest of us can go hang! We need change!"

Esther nodded and held up a hand. Impressively, she got silence. "Tomorrow, I will return and begin my campaign in earnest to be your mayor." She pointed at one then another and another in the crowd. "I hope I can count on *your* votes. It's high time that certain coincidences stopped happening in our town!"

The women, and even some of the men, applauded.

A man at the back leaned down and picked up a sizeable rock.

Cash eased his horse to the man's side and nudged Paint's flank against him. "Sorry, Mister." The man's face twisted in anger then his eyes caught the U.S. Marshal badge. He dropped the rock. "Wise move, sir." Cash put a finger to the brim of his hat.

* * *

As they rode out of town, Cash said, "You seemed to be getting on with that young girl, Danny. What's her name?"

Esther chuckled. "You don't miss much, do you?"

Alongside her, Danny reddened. "Ada … Well, she's named Adela but likes to be called Ada."

"She's a nice girl," Esther said. "Comes from a hardworking family."

"Yes. I like her very much," Danny said and glanced away, embarrassed.

Cash changed the subject. "And, Esther, it seems you connected with many in that crowd. Sounds like they're ready for change."

She bit her lip and then shrugged. "Maybe."

"You don't seem too pleased. I mean, apart from one fool stooping to pick up a rock, I didn't detect any animosity."

"A man picked up a rock?" she queried. Her complexion paled.

"He dropped it when I pointed out his error."

She smiled fleetingly, but her mood didn't lift.

"What's happened?" he asked.

"The printer said my posters would be ready today. But I can't have them, even though I've paid good money for them. They've been confiscated by the sheriff!"

"That lets us know where Sheriff Hain stands, I guess."

"It's so frustrating! They want me to fight this election with a hand tied behind my back. But they can't silence me—even if they send killers." She glanced at him. "When I left the undertaker's, I overheard you making some arrangement with Mr. Peel. What was it?"

"A little advertising," Cash said. "Might bring in something of interest."

She wrinkled her brow. "You've grown more mysterious over the years, I see."

"I learned to gamble, Esther."

"Cards close to your chest, is that it?"

"Partly. Also, I gamble with lives—all the time."

She turned away, as if shaken by his cold response.

Their return journey was uneventful, though Cash never relaxed his wariness, and they hardly spoke. Cash guessed she was mulling over what to do next. If she was having second thoughts about contesting for mayor, he couldn't blame her. Though he never reckoned her for a quitter, either.

By the time they got back to the ranch, it was dark.

Cash told them both to stay with the buckboard while he dismounted, Colt drawn. He crossed over to the porch and lit the lantern hanging there, then checked inside the ranch house and the bunkhouse. Apparently, according to Esther, the two hands she'd employed upped and left about a week ago—without picking up their wages. She and Danny had been alone out here for seven days. Cash wondered why those against her waited so long.

"All clear!" he called, holstering his gun.

"Right, I'll get some food ready," Esther said, jumping down from the buckboard. "Danny, please see to the horses. Cash, you can bunk down in the spare room."

"Maybe I should sleep in the bunkhouse—seeing you might be mayor soon," he suggested.

She laughed. "I don't pay no mind to talk. You're my bodyguard. You're after villains, not my body." She smiled and patted his cheek. "Besides, my son's a good chaperone."

Cash returned her smile, thinking on those distant yet fond memories.

After a good supper of griddled pork, onions and potatoes, he retired to bed, his six-gun stuffed under his pillow. Niggling thoughts about dates, birthdays and timing nagged at him until he fell asleep.

* * *

Over a breakfast of ham, eggs and beans, washed down with hot black coffee, Cash listened as Esther filled in some blanks.

When she opted to run for mayor, it seemed that the town was divided. "To begin with, it was obvious that no one took me serious." She grinned. "But as the ballot day got nearer, I realized that against all so-called experts' predictions, I was becoming popular."

"Why was that?" Cash asked.

She shrugged. "I guess I was outspoken about the existing administration."

"I can imagine," he said with a smile. "Is that when you started receiving threatening letters?"

She nodded and waved a hand in dismissal. "All politicians get them. It's part of the deal, I suppose. Cranks, mostly."

"But some of them were a mite serious, right?"

"Yes. They turned dark and wrote like they knew how Dean died ..."

"So, whoever killed your husband could write, at least."

"That's not remotely funny, Cash."

"I didn't mean it to be. But we've got to eliminate those who probably aren't responsible."

"Very well." She let out a short laugh. "I bet right now they wish they'd killed me when they shot Dean."

Cash started. "You were there, at the killing?"

She nodded. "Yes. I gave Sheriff Hain a good description of the pair. The idiots even said their names as they gunned down Dean. One was called Jack, the other Vim."

"Do you want to tell me what happened?"

She lowered her eyes and studied her hands, which rested on the tabletop. "Dean and I had just come out of the saloon. A lovely singer—Pearl Courtney—was passing through, and gave the town a rendition of some songs from *Die Fledermaus*." She made no move to wipe away the tears that streamed down her face. "She sang of love and loss, and injustice, would you believe?" She pulled out a handkerchief and blew her nose, still ignoring the tears.

She and Dean had stepped out of the side entrance, into the alley—the only way to leave without shoving their way through the packed and odoriferous audience.

"I thought it was just chance—that's what Sheriff Hain said, anyway."

Two ruffians accosted them, guns leveled. Demanded they give up their valuables. Dean protested, said when he was mayor, there'd be no place for the likes of them. One of them grabbed at Esther's pearl necklace and it broke, scattering pearls everywhere. Dean lunged forward, and shouted, "Leave my wife alone!"

Suddenly, they both fired at him.

"Got what you wanted, Mister—now she's alone—a widow!"

In that instant, Esther went wild, grabbing a discarded length of timber, and attacked them.

"I distinctly remember the tall thin one saying, 'Don't shoot her, Jack. We were told to leave her be.' The other one—he had an eye-patch—he said, 'Damn you, Vim, I told you not to use my name … Oh, hell, let's go.'" She shrugged. "They ran off, without even taking Dean's wallet."

"They weren't the brightest villains, were they?"

"No, but deadly enough. By the time I turned to Dean, he only had a few words for me … private words."

"So, Dean was killed by order, but you were deliberately left alone?"

"It was only after that I wondered about that."

"What conclusions did you make?"

"I wasn't a threat to the mayoral campaign. I was a little woman, of no consequence."

Cash whistled. "Little did they know."

She dabbed at her eyes. "The townspeople were full of sympathy. Wanted to erect a fine marble headstone with statues of angels for Dean in Boot Hill. I declined, said I'd bury him at the ranch, where he belonged."

"What did Sheriff Hain do about the shooting?"

"Not a lot. He didn't press his enquiries too much."

"And the sheriff is hired by the mayor?"

"Oh, yes, in this town, that's how they go about it," she replied bitterly. "And now he's confiscated my posters."

* * *

Mayor Brett Nolan paced the floor in his ranch house. From time to time, he glared sideways at Sheriff Hain, his insurance, and Lance Jacobson, his friend. "Having that Marshal here isn't good, Sheriff," he growled.

"You're stating the obvious, sir. But there isn't much I can do about it."

"Why don't you just get rid of him?" Jacobson said.

Nolan stopped pacing. "Because they'd send another damned pronto, that's why. Isn't that so, Sheriff?"

"I reckon, Mr. Mayor."

Mrs. Angelina Nolan entered with a silver tray of coffee and cups. She smiled, her strawberry-red painted lips and rouged cheeks more suitable to the dance hall than the mayor's parlor. She leaned forward, offering a view of her décolletage that engaged her guests, and placed the tray on the coffee table between the men. "The good marshal could always meet up with an accident."

"Thank you, dear, for that insightful contribution," Nolan said, and sat at the sofa opposite the other two.

Angelina poured coffee into the cups. "We are fresh out of milk, so black will have to do."

"It's the only black I favor," said Jacobson with a wink.

"You're too partial for your own good, Lance," she replied, a hand patting her dark brown hair.

"Angelina isn't so fussy, she'll do business with anyone," Nolan said, "as long as she gets what she wants."

Husband and wife smiled at each other, suggesting marital harmony. Nolan reckoned both Hain and Jacobson were fooled, anyway. Truth was, of late Angelina had become bored with being wife to the mayor. She craved excitement. And he wondered if he didn't provide it, she'd stray somewhere else where she could obtain it, and he could go hang.

He sipped at the hot coffee. Things were looking bleak, and he didn't understand it. He'd bought and paid for many votes, but word was out that the majority of voting women were against him and, according to Angelina, many of them were already starting to nag their husbands to vote their way too. Despite their rocky marriage arrangement, he had to credit her with political loyalty, if not wifely constancy.

Angelina was one of his staunchest supporters and just as ruthless as him.

Idly eyeing her now, he wondered with whom she dallied. He felt sure that it wasn't either of the two men in the room.

Nolan knew what rancher Jacobson believed when it came to women—they should cook and bear children. That's all they were good for. He'd had two wives, overworked and buried both. He had two sons, Matt and Jerry, one from each wife, and both were entirely different in temperament. He promised his support in the elections. Nolan dismissed the very thought of Jacobson being the man who cuckolded him.

As far as Sheriff Hain, Nolan knew the man owed his job to him. Hain had too much to lose to dally with his sponsor's wife. Although Hain didn't know it, Nolan was aware of the sheriff's little extra earners—especially the protection racket he ran, fleecing the various immigrant shopkeepers. Yet Hain's money was never evident in his appearance. Maybe he was saving it for a rainy day, putting it in the bank.

Then there was the bank manager, Martin Plampin. That smooth bastard tended to sit on the political fence. More than once he told Nolan that he couldn't see the point of women owning a bank account, since very few ran businesses or put money in his bank. He allowed there was the occasional exception, such as Mrs. Tolliver and Ma Bartleby, the madam of the whorehouse. Plampin's business survived because of the men who banked with him. Nolan had a sneaking suspicion that Plampin had a soft spot for Ma Bartleby, which might not bode well, since that harridan was siding with Mrs. Tolliver. Mighty strange, that—Mrs. Bartleby used her women, all of them indentured to pay off their contracts, but was willing to give them a vote. Maybe he'd have to get Sheriff Hain to fine her for some moral transgression or other trifling misdemeanor; that would put her in her place.

He glanced at Hain. "Anything new to report?"

"I paid Horton Eldridge a visit." Hain smiled.

Up until now, Nolan thought he'd bought an ideal lawman—obedient and willing to turn a blind eye when asked. Hain's inability to deal with the U.S. Marshal caused him concern, however. For now, he'd give him the benefit of the doubt. "So, what did Eldridge have to say?"

"He had the posters all printed up for Mrs. Tolliver. She was due in to collect them today."

"Really?"

Hain nodded, evidently enjoying his moment in the limelight. "I told him I'd have to confiscate the lot." He shook his head and chuckled. "He wasn't too pleased about that. 'They're likely to inflame emotions,' I says, 'and cause a disturbance of the peace.' He argued that she'd paid for them—and he'd spent time and money printing them. 'Then, she's out of pocket,' I told him. 'Evidence of sedition,' I said."

Nolan laughed while Angelina clapped her hands, her red nails quite pointed. "Well done, Sheriff, that's marvelous!"

"Thanks kindly. The posters are in the jail outhouse, the best use I could think of for them."

"Brilliant!" Nolan turned to his wife. "Dear, I think our coffees would benefit from a little stiffening—the best whiskey, perhaps?"

Obediently, she rose and with a swish of skirts walked over to the sideboard and opened a bottle. With utmost finesse, she moved among them, dispensing liquor into their cups.

Nolan raised his cup. "Here's to the election, gentlemen."

Angelina poured her whiskey direct into a tumbler and swigged it back, her pert nose raised. "And may the Devil confound the Tolliver woman at every turn."

"Amen to that, my dear," Mayor Nolan said.

* * *

The two hired ruffians—Jack Wexler and Vim Portland— were paid off by Nolan and told to get out of town, since the widow could identify them. After their departure, Nolan had pushed his luck by hiring Ash Devlin and Tiny Pucket. They were supposed to do away with Tolliver and her son, maybe burn them in a fire that could look like an accident. Instead, they got themselves killed by that damned marshal.

Nolan realized he could not afford to hire any more killers. He'd watched Mrs. Tolliver haranguing that crowd. If she met an untimely end now, suspicion would fall on him. With a U.S. Marshal around, it wouldn't pay to mess up. Especially as he knew there were moves afoot to make Wyoming a state. That could be the beginning of something really big for him.

He must think of something else to ensure Mrs. Tolliver came second in the two-horse race for mayor.

CHAPTER 3

Making an Impression

Bear Ridge was twenty miles southeast of Bear Pines, and about the same size. Cash had been reluctant to leave Esther and Danny, but she dismissed his concerns with ease. "Your journey's most necessary to my campaign, Cash, and you know it. Danny'll look out for me, be sure." She promised that they'd be vigilant and always keep loaded guns to hand.

"I'll be back in a couple of days, at the most," he promised.

For a moment, she hesitated, as if about to give him a peck on the cheek, then she smiled and waved him off.

As he rode away, he was tempted to look back at the mother and son—but he didn't. His back itched some. He wondered if he was being watched. Maybe the mayor was just waiting for him to ride off?

No, surely he wouldn't be so stupid as to try killing Esther a third time. Then again, most villains were stupid.

Within an hour, he'd dismissed the Tollivers from his mind. He hoped there might be some useful information to glean from the people in Bear Ridge. He reckoned that Dean

Tolliver's killers wouldn't run far, particularly if they were paid. They'd be tempted to blackmail their employer or maybe wait for similar work. Of course, they could have gone in a totally different direction.

His first stop was the sheriff's office.

Ed Kaye was in his fifties but seemed capable enough. His two young deputies were in their twenties and did all the patrolling of the town. "I do the gun work, my deputies do the police work." He shrugged. "It seems to suit. My town's quiet, even on weekends."

"Glad to hear it," Cash said. "I'm looking for two men suspected of murder." He gave Esther's description of Jack and Vim. "Don't know their surnames."

Kaye nodded. "Sounds like Jack Wexler and Vim Portland."

Cash could hardly believe his luck: pay-dirt on his first try. "Where can I find them?"

Sheriff Kaye stood up. "I'll give you a hand. Wexler's a mean son of a bitch."

"No, Sheriff. I'd like to talk to them by myself, if that's all right with you."

Kaye sat back. "Okay. So long as you don't go shooting my town full of holes while you do your talking."

"I'll tread easy."

"Well …" Kaye squinted at the large clock above the entrance door to the cells. "About this time of day, you'll find Jack Wexler in the saloon—two blocks down, the Plugged Nickel. For two or three weeks now he's been spending money like it was going out of fashion."

"For him, it just might be true," Cash said.

"Yeah, I suppose there's a shortage of the green stuff in prison ... Well, now, Vim Portland's a different sort altogether. He's a hard worker who tends to get led astray. You'll find him out at the Maddison place, helping with a new build, a stone ranch house."

"Is Maddison important 'round here, then?"

"He owns this town," said Kaye. "But he don't own me. In fact, I've found him a fair and reasonable man. Turned down the offer of mayor. Said it should go to a more worthy person. He was right, too. Rowan Slateman, the newspaper editor, was voted in and he's doing all right. Stands up to Brett Nolan whenever there's any intertown dispute, too."

"Glad to hear it. How do I get to Maddison's?"

"Take the east trail out of town, follow the road for about six miles and take the right-hand fork. Their ranch house is about two miles down that track."

"Thanks, Sheriff."

"Don't mention it."

Next, Cash called at Slateman, the printer's, which also served as the home of the town's newspaper, *The Ridge Times*. The sign in the door said *Open*, so he did and walked in. A tinkling bell announced his presence.

The man behind the reception desk glanced up. He wore a stained printer's apron, a striped shirt and a cap with eyeshade. His fingers appeared permanently discolored by the ink.

"Mr. Slateman?" Cash inquired.

He nodded. "What can I do for you, mister—ah, sorry, marshal?"

"Could you print up thirty of these posters today—in an hour or two? And fifty of these leaflets?" He handed over two sheets that Esther had given him.

Slateman studied the papers and nodded. "Sure. Not much type, short and to the point. Though I don't see why Mrs. Tolliver didn't get it done by Mr. Eldridge, the printer in her own town."

"It's kinda political."

Slateman grinned. "I'll say it is. You know, quite a few people in this town will be curious to see how Bear Pines vote. It might prove interesting."

"It's already more interesting than some townspeople want," Cash said.

"I'd say." Slateman glanced at his fob. "Give me two hours, marshal. Is that all right?"

"Sure. I'll be back."

* * *

The road to the Maddison spread was easy to follow. He crossed a narrow wooden bridge over a stream, something the sheriff had neglected to mention. He reached the entrance gate at about eleven o'clock.

As he rode up, he noted there were at least six people working on the new two-story ranch house. Two wagons filled with wooden beams stood idle to the right, while four sections of preformed gable ends leaned against the barn on the left.

The broad chimneybreast was half complete at the right-hand end. A thin man and a stocky fellow balanced on a wooden platform halfway up the chimney, busily scooping cement from a big trough and laying large stone blocks into the structure. Far over on his right flowed the stream he'd crossed on his way here.

Another two men wore aprons with pouches for nails and carried claw hammers. They were walking from the barn to the porch area when they both noticed Cash. They stopped and glanced toward the old, single-story ranch house that was set back over on their left.

A man on the roof called, "Who you looking for, stranger? This is private property."

Cash eased back his jacket, showed his badge. "I've got a few questions for Mr. Vim Portland. Can you point him out?"

"Can't it wait? We're busy, as you can see."

"No, it can't wait." He reined in at the porch and looped the reins round the hitching rail. He craned his neck and shouted, "This is a murder inquiry." He dismounted and waited. At the porch doorway rested two rifles—a Marlin .40-60 and a Winchester M1876—and a Parker shotgun. He glimpsed inside, surprised to note that, unlike most ranch houses, the floor here was a solid expanse of cement. The smoothed-over area was still wet and glistened.

"Murder, eh?"

At risk of getting a crick in his neck, Cash looked up. The man walked along the topmost beam, balancing like an acrobat. He reached the righthand end, overlooking the chimney. "You've got half an hour," he called down to the thin worker. "If you're not finished by then, don't come back!"

"Right, boss."

With remarkable agility, Vim Portland swung off the platform, his feet connecting with a flimsy ladder and then he ran down to the ground. He strode confidently across the hard-baked earth. "What's this about a murder, Marshal?"

Portland was tall, with rusty-colored hair and a slight squint in his left eye. He smiled, his teeth prominent and white. He strongly resembled the description Esther provided, yet seemed untroubled at facing a deputy U.S. Marshal.

"I've got an eyewitness statement that places you in the alley when Mr. Dean Tolliver was shot dead."

"Me?" Portland laughed. "I haven't been anywhere near Bear Pines for months."

"Who said anything about Bear Pines?"

Portland's smile froze and his gray eyes shifted slightly. Then he grinned. "We've all read about the murder, Marshal. It ain't exactly a secret, is it?"

"No …" Nonchalantly, Cash removed a cheroot and lit it. "Where were you when the murder occurred?"

"Hell, I have trouble remembering where I was yesterday, so I couldn't say where I was three—four weeks back."

"You remember the murder was three or four weeks ago, though?" Cash blew smoke out the corner of his mouth.

"Sure, it was in the papers. I told you."

"So you did." Cash fished inside his shirt, pulled out a sheet of paper. "This is my witness's statement. Care to read it, tell me if she was mistaken?" He thrust it at the man.

Portland looked at it and his eyes scanned over the handwritten sheet. Then he handed it back. "Seems all right, I guess. Don't know why she thinks it was me in that alley."

54

"This happens to be my usual list of supplies I fall back on when I head into mountain country."

"Oh?"

"You were holding the sheet upside down."

"Ah, well …"

"You can't read, can you?"

Portland glanced away and then back. "That ain't a crime, Marshal. Leastways, not that I know of."

"So, you didn't read about Mr. Tolliver's murder in the newspaper, did you?"

"No. Didn't say I did. I said it was in the papers. Zeke read it out to me over supper. Yeah, it was Zeke."

"I must have a word with Zeke, then. Just to corroborate your story."

Portland shrugged. "I don't know why you bother. It's circum—circumcise …"

"Circumstantial?"

"Yeah, that's it."

Cash shook his head. "It really amazes me how so many criminals can hardly read or write their name, but they know their way around the law like they'd studied it for years!"

"Just because I can't read, don't mean I ain't smart."

"If you're so smart, why do you run around with Jack Wexler?"

"J-Jack Who?"

Cash shook his head. "I think we've done this before."

Portland grinned. "Just my little joke, Marshal."

"The joke's on you, then. You see, Jack talked." Lying often got results. "Said you shot Dean Tolliver twice, while he stood and watched, holding onto Mrs. Tolliver."

Portland's face suddenly turned deep red and his jaw tightened. "That lying, double-crossing swine!" Abruptly, he ducked and swerved back, making for the porch area.

Cash followed, his half-smoked cheroot sticking out the corner of his mouth. For a fleeting second, he was tempted to draw and shoot, but firing on a moving man was risky; he couldn't guarantee he'd only wing him or get a leg. He needed Portland alive. He wanted him and Wexler to reveal who hired them.

Portland clattered onto the porch boards and reached down for a rifle.

Cash charged up the steps and rammed his shoulder into Portland's legs.

They fell through the open doorway and landed on the slippery, slimy cement floor. Immediately, they both sank into the gray ooze.

Portland was under him, submerged, frantically flaying his hands, the rifle forgotten. Cash pulled back an instant before he fell face-first into the wet cement.

He lurched to his feet, ungainly, the weight of the liquid quite surprising, tugging at his limbs. Once he gained firm footing at the base, he desperately reached down and groped for Portland's hands, which had stopped moving. He heaved, accompanied by a sucking sound, and finally fell back onto the threshold of the wooden porch, Portland on top of him with mouth, nostrils and eye sockets cement-filled.

Cash turned Portland on his side and thrust his fingers into the man's mouth. He levered out viscous clods of the stuff, but to no avail.

He stood, grabbing the doorjamb for support.

"What the hell's happened here?" barked the boss from the base of the porch steps.

Cash wiped his face with the back of his hand. "Clearly, Portland cemented his relationship with his final job," he said.

CHAPTER 4

Finger Trouble

Cash stood in the shallows of the stream, his shirt drying on a boulder. Water swirled round his boots while he washed off the cement from the front of his pants. His muscles rippled in the sunlight.

"So, you're the troublemaker who made a mess of our floor?"

Cash glanced up, uncaring. He'd heard the horse approach, the bridle chinking, the swish of skirts. His gun-belt was nearby on another boulder, but he saw no call to reach for it. "I presume you must be Mrs. Maddison, ma'am?"

She sat astride a handsome chestnut and wore a green serge riding skirt and brown suede jacket. Her tan hat was tipped back from her forehead, her auburn hair hanging loose to her shoulders. "You haven't answered my question," she said, pointing at Cash with her horsewhip, "so I don't feel inclined to answer yours."

"Well, sure, I contributed to the mess, I reckon," he answered, amused at her tone. He shook his head in mock regret. "It's most unfortunate, ma'am, but one of your workmen was wanted by the law, and he didn't fancy surrendering peaceably."

"It seems he surrendered his life."

"That wasn't my intention, I wanted him alive to testify in court."

"Ah, yes, our foreman told me you're a U.S. Marshal."

"Indeed. Cash Laramie, ma'am." He bowed slightly. "And you are?"

"Miss Jane Maddison. Daughter of Roger, the landowner here." She gestured with her arm to encompass pretty much what they could see of the valley.

"That's a lot of land for one man."

"It's family land, not just one man's, Marshal."

"If you'll indulge me a little longer, Miss Maddison, I'd like to wash off the rest of this darned cement. If it stays and sets, it'll weigh heavily on my horse." He raised a hand to stay any comment. "Then I'll be gone—off your family's land."

"Which includes this stream."

"And a real pretty stream it is, too." He moved closer, grinned up at her. "Most suitable for laundry work."

"I find you rather insolent, Marshal."

Cash smiled and reached up, grabbed her arm and tugged her off the horse. In one swift motion, he flung her into the center of the stream, away from any out-jutting rocks. "And I find you a mite too haughty for your own good, Miss Maddison."

Spluttering, she stood, while water gushed off her. Her hazel eyes flashed as she righted the hat on her drenched head. "How dare you!"

"I dare almost anything. That's what living's all about."

She raised her horsewhip and then seemed to think better of it. Then, arms akimbo, she burst out laughing.

Despite himself, Cash grinned. "What's so funny?"

"Me," she said between laughs. "I must look a sight!"

"I reckon you look real fine in those wet clothes, Miss Jane."

Ignoring his compliment, she tucked stray lank hair behind an ear. "Your name, Cash, it's rather odd, isn't it?"

"It pays."

She licked her lips, openly appraising his face and torso. "Yes, I daresay it does," she said and offered her hand.

He helped her out of the stream.

When she attained the dry ground at the edge, she seemed reluctant to let go of his hand. "Do you throw all your women into streams, Cash?"

"Not all," he replied. "And I don't recall claiming you as one of 'my women.'"

She pressed a hand on his chest, her wide hazel eyes on his, her full lips slightly parted. "I've said it for you, I guess."

* * *

Angelina Nolan rolled over, smiling at the feel of the grass against her bare flesh. Prudently, she had divested herself of all clothes to avoid telltale grass and dirt stains. She smiled to herself. She enjoyed being wanton. Playing with that word, she smiled and whispered, "I'm wantin' more."

Jerry Jacobson leaned over her, his lean features creased in a smile. His deep blue eyes feasted on her. "You'll have to wait, I'm all spent."

"Cashed up, you might say?" she purred.

"Eh?"

"A play on words, my love. I was thinking of that marshal. Such an odd name—Cash."

"Don't mention his name, especially while we're … well, doing this."

Letting out a mew, she wrapped her arms and legs around him. "You're so forceful, Jerry. I like that in a man."

"Is that why you're with me right now and not your husband?"

She chuckled, nibbled his ear. "Brett is a good mayor and businessman, but he hasn't got your stamina."

"When are you going to tell him about us?" he asked.

"After the election. When he's been elected mayor again, he'll be happy enough. I'll make the break then."

He twirled his fingers in her dark brown hair. "You mean our future happiness depends on him winning?"

"Yes, it does. I couldn't leave him if he lost. He'd be a doubly broken man."

Jerry sighed and stroked her breasts. "Then we'd better hope he wins."

As she ministered to him and he became aroused, despite his earlier protests, she whispered, "I think we can do more than hope, darling Jerry. I'd like to think you could perhaps upset the balance a little." She rocked over him, tantalizing, arousing herself with the movement.

"Balance?"

"That interfering marshal—you know, if he was out of the way, I think Mrs. Tolliver might back down."

"But he's a U.S. Marshal."

"He's a man—just like you," she whispered, raking her fingers through his fair hair. "Though I bet not as much of a man as you, oh, no, not nearly as much …"

* * *

The Plugged Nickel resembled virtually all other saloons Cash had frequented. He wondered how many he'd walked into over the years. Too many to count. And in a good portion of them he'd faced death and, in a few others, disillusion.

It looked as though some drinkers were starting early: it was just past one in the afternoon, yet six men leaned over the bar counter, each in his own little world, studying his whiskey glass.

Jack Wexler stood next to a piano, his right hand on the edge of the keyboard, the other resting on the shoulder of the blonde female pianist. Wexler's blind side was on the left, so he couldn't see anyone who entered the saloon. Perhaps he didn't care. He only had an eye for the piano player, it seemed.

"What'll it be …?" The barkeep's words floundered when he noticed the badge.

Cash strode across the floor and stood behind the pianist. "Jack Wexler, I'm a U.S. Marshal."

Wexler flinched, removed his hand from the woman's shoulder and the pianist swiveled round on her stool, showing a lot of leg.

"So?" Wexler said, his one eye squinting. "Am I supposed to be impressed?"

"So … I'm here to arrest you on suspicion of the murder of Dean Tolliver."

The woman pianist must have been a contortionist at some time in her life. In seconds, she slid from the stool, scrabbled past Wexler and bustled off to the left.

"Dean Who?" Wexler said, sniggering.

"You know who," Cash snapped and lunged forward. He slammed the piano lid down, crushing Wexler's fingers in the gap. In the same smooth movement, he lifted Wexler's Smith & Wesson from the holster on his right hip.

Wexler squealed like a stuck pig. "My fingers!"

Cash lifted the lid and rasped a hand over his stubble. "What's left of them."

"That's my gun hand," Wexler moaned, his solitary eye glaring.

"Where you're going, I don't think you'll be allowed a gun. Consider yourself lucky. Your pal Vim is dead."

Wexler paled.

"Now, we need to have a little talk before we get to Bear Pines."

"I've got nothing to say," Wexler croaked.

"Wouldn't you like to think so."

CHAPTER 5

A Date with the Undertaker

Cash collected the batch of posters and leaflets in their roll of cloth and tied them behind the cantle of his saddle. He checked and tightened the cinch then walked round to make sure that Wexler's saddle was secure too. Wexler's hands were tethered with piggin' string to the horn and his grulla's reins were looped to Cash's saddle horn. Cash always carried plenty of piggin' string, since he never knew when he'd need to truss up the odd varmint—and they didn't come much odder than Wexler.

"If you want, Marshal, you can keep Wexler in the cells overnight," offered Sheriff Kaye. "I'd be glad of your company."

"Thanks, Sheriff, but no. I need to get back." He swung up onto Paint. "It ain't far."

Kaye leaned against the boardwalk post. "Shame about Portland, he might've made something of himself if he hadn't been so easily led by scum like Wexler."

Cash adjusted his Stetson. The sun was low on the horizon. "The secret is, don't get led, I guess. Be a leader, instead."

"Easier said than done, Marshal. Not everyone's a leader, you know."

"I reckon not." They shook hands. "Thanks for the coffee and the hospitality. You've got a fine little town here."

At that moment, Jane Maddison rode up. Now, she wore a dun-colored riding skirt and a buckskin jacket over a white blouse. "Going so soon, Marshal?"

Cash doffed his hat. "Duty calls, Miss Maddison."

"And you're a man who lives to do his duty."

"Yes, I guess I do. It's the right thing to do, I reckon."

"Well," she said, "it was a pleasure meeting you."

"Likewise." He moved the two horses out.

"Come again," she called.

"I mean to," he replied and waved, heading out of town.

They made good time on their fresh horses. When they were about five miles out, Cash noted several trees a few yards off from the road. He said, "We'll make camp for the night among those trees."

"I thought you told the sheriff we were going direct to Bear Pines."

"I changed my mind."

Wexler didn't seem too happy about it. A short while later, he was even less happy as he hung upside down over a fire. "You can't do this," he wheezed and then coughed.

"I'll do whatever it takes to get your confession, Wexler."

"I can't write!"

"Then dictate it to me."

"Dic-what?"

"Tell me in your own words and I'll write them down."

Wexler coughed again. "You could make up anything. Who's to say it was true?"

Cash laughed. "I guess Portland learned it from you, all the ways to wriggle like a crooked lawyer."

"Yeah, well, my so-called confession ain't worth a damn unless it's got a witness." Wexler spat into the fire. "So go to hell!"

"Not me, friend. It's you." Cash pointed at the flames. "And it seems to me you're pretty damn close already!"

Ten minutes later, his singed hair glinting with a few red sparks, Wexler screamed, "Stop it, damn you, Marshal! I'll tell you everything!"

Cash batted the sparks with his hand and pulled Wexler down. The vile smell brought back unpleasant memories of burned homesteads and corpses. "Tell the truth," he warned, "or I'll hoist you up there again—and I might just leave you next time."

"I won't lie to you, Marshal, honest."

Between sips of coffee, Wexler slowly related what happened in the dark alley adjoining the saloon.

When Cash finished writing, he tethered Wexler to the bole of the tree from which he'd been suspended.

Wexler said with a grin, "Still ain't worth a damn without a witness' signature."

"That's why *I'm* here," Jane Maddison said. She stepped out of the dark shadows beyond the campfire, leading her chestnut horse.

"What the hell?" Wexler swore and the blood drained from his face.

"The marshal suggested I follow so I could witness your confession." She eyed Wexler with distaste. "Frankly, having heard it, I wish he'd boiled your brains. You don't deserve to live, Mr. Wexler."

Without a word, Cash handed her the statement sheet, and she used his pen and ink to sign as a witness. He countersigned.

"Now," she said, rubbing her hands together, "I'd like some hot coffee. It got a mite chilly sitting out there in the dark."

"Sure, Miss Maddison." Cash smiled. "And in a little while, I'll see if I can arrange to warm you up once I've settled our criminal someplace else to ensure our privacy."

"That would be greatly appreciated, Marshal."

* * *

Next morning at dawn, Cash led Wexler with the man's feet tied to his stirrups. "Just so you don't get any funny ideas about jumping off and running, Cash said. Jane Maddison rode alongside him.

About an hour out from the camp, apparently on impulse, she leaned across the space between them and whispered, "You're just as exciting when you're dry, you know?"

He kissed her, briefly, and squinted as sunlight glinted off his badge—no, it wasn't his badge ....

A bullet hit Jane in the forehead. Her blood splashed in Cash's face and she tumbled from her horse. A second bullet smashed into Wexler's chest and he slumped in his saddle.

Between the first and second shots, Cash snatched his Yellow Boy from its scabbard and slipped off Paint, putting the horse between himself and the shooter. He landed on his feet and scuttled behind Wexler's whickering horse.

He glanced at Jane. Her eyes stared up into the sky, unblinking. Wexler groaned, heaving in air, swearing on blood-flecked lips, as his hands clasped his saddle horn. The man was dying, but he might still prove useful.

Cash squatted and peered under the legs of Wexler's horse. A cluster of boulders about two hundred yards ahead probably hid the shooter.

With patient prods, gentle whispers and coaxing, he eased the horse in the direction of the boulders while two more slugs pounded into Wexler.

Cash rested his rifle on Wexler's saddlebows and fired four times, as fast as he could work the lever of the Yellow Boy. The bullets ricocheted off the boulders.

He got no response. Odd.

Jacking another shell into the chamber, he continued to use Wexler and his horse as a shield, walking the animal at an angle toward the boulders.

The horse seemed to settle down, despite the ever-present smell of blood from its rider. Yet Cash still tasted Jane's on his mouth—a mouth that a few minutes ago had kissed her lips.

When he got to the boulders, he clambered over and round them cautiously, sweat soaking his back. The bushwhacker had fled, leaving four empty shell casings— .40-60 caliber. The tracks of the bushwhacker's horse revealed a deformed shoe on the front, left forehoof.

When Cash got back, Wexler was still slumped in the saddle, but dead. Good riddance. He used the man's lariat to secure him in that position then moved slowly over to Jane Maddison.

He slung Jane's body over her horse and fastened her there, and reflected on some words Esther had said all those years ago: "You know, young man, you've got those good looks that'll always draw women. I reckon you'll be quite the lady-killer."

Prophetic words, though not in the way she meant them. How many women had he known who'd been killed? Sometimes, even in his presence. He draped his blanket over her body and tied it down so she'd be covered.

* * *

Cash rode into Bear Pines and noted that several citizens stopped on the boardwalk to stare at his grim little caravan. He reined in at the sheriff's office and Hain rose from his rocker.

"What the hell have you got there, Marshal?"

"Two bodies—one's Wexler. The other's Miss Jane Maddison."

Hain swore. "The Maddison girl? Hell, what happened?"

"We were bushwhacked. I'll tell you about it later. Can you send one of your deputies out to the Maddison place? Jane's father needs to be told."

"Yeah, sure." Hain turned on his heel and bellowed into the open office door, "Burt, get on out here, I've got an important errand for you!"

A lanky deputy emerged. "What is it, Sheriff?"

Hain explained and the deputy left for the livery.

"Couldn't you find the other one?" Hain asked.

"Portland?"

"Yeah, that's the one."

"He died resisting arrest."

"That's a shame."

"Yes, for them it is." Cash refrained from asking how Sheriff Hain knew Wexler and Portland. Until now, he'd appeared ignorant of their existence. Esther had only overheard their first names. "Can you arrange for the undertaker to move them to his place?"

"Sure." Again, Hain turned and shouted. "Zeke, get on out here—you've got a date with the undertaker."

Zeke, portly and normally of ruddy complexion, emerged with his face pale and drawn. "Undertaker's, Sheriff?"

While Sheriff Hain explained, Cash dismounted, tied Paint to the rail and made his way along the boardwalk, grateful for the shade provided by the roof.

He stopped outside Peel's Emporium for the Deceased. The bodies of Ash and Tiny occupied two coffins, upended against the wall. A placard above each stated, *If you know who these men are, contact U.S. Marshal Laramie at Judge McPiece's house.* A definite foul miasma hovered around the corpses, along with a small cloud of black flies. He detected movement in the corner of Ash's left eye—a maggot, probably.

He'd check with the judge in a minute. For now, he needed a drink to wash away the dust and the blood.

Pausing outside the saloon, he noted a golden-brown Chickasaw, its rear leg hipshot while it stood at the rail. Sticking out of the leather scabbard was a rifle butt—a Marlin .40-60. He stepped down and gently approached the horse. After a moment of familiarity, the animal let him lift

71

the front, left foot. The deformed shoe was unmistakable. He examined the saddle—the initials JJ burned into its leather flap.

Easing his clenched jaw, Cash licked his lips and turned toward the saloon. He thirsted, but it suddenly wasn't for whiskey.

He swung open the batwings.

There was a general murmur from the eight customers in the room—two at the bar, and four at one table and two at another. The barkeep gave Cash a quick glance and something in Cash's face must have decided his next move: he backed toward the far end of the bar, away from his clientele.

Moving to one side of the entrance, Cash asked in a loud voice, "Who owns the Chickasaw?"

Silence fell.

All eyes were on him.

"I want to know who owns that horse."

"That's my horse, Marshal." A handsome fair-haired man in his early twenties stood at his table, while his three companions slid their chairs back, their eyes never leaving Cash.

He noted that they were all armed.

"What's your name, Mister?" Cash demanded.

"Jerry Jacobson." He gestured at a dark-haired man of similar age. "That's my brother, Matt." Matt stood up slowly, eyes narrowed, his hand hovering near the butt of his six-gun, and nodded.

"Let's you and me go outside, Jerry, and talk," Cash said.

"I don't think so, Marshal," Jerry said. "If you have anything to say, you can say it in front of my brother and our friends and neighbors."

Cash shrugged. "It's all the same to me, son."

"I ain't your son, Marshal."

Ignoring this comment, Cash said, "Have you loaned out your horse today?"

Jerry Jacobson grinned. "Loaned out?" He laughed. "No way!"

His brother and the others laughed, briefly.

"In which case, I'm arresting you for the murder of Jack Wexler and Jane Maddison."

"Jane Maddison?" Matt lifted a hand, grabbed his brother's arm. "You never said anything about—"

"Shut it, Matt!" Jerry snarled.

"But …"

Jerry shrugged off his brother's hand and went for his pistol.

Cash cleared leather and fired.

His gun pointing at the floorboards, Jerry backed into the table and stared at his bloody belly.

"Jerry!" Matt's fingers closed on his gun.

"Matt, don't do it," Cash warned, pointing the smoking barrel of his Colt at the man.

His face crumpled in concern, Matt left his six-gun alone and rushed over to his brother. "You bastard, you've killed him."

Cash shook his head. "He isn't dead yet, though he deserves to be." He turned to one of the white-faced men at their table. "Go get the doctor. He might survive a gut shot, he might not … Depends on how good your doc is."

Tears streamed down Matt's cheeks. "Damn you, you don't care, do you?"

"Your brother killed two people this morning." Cash shrugged. "He didn't much care about snuffing out their lives. Why should I worry about his?"

"Bastard!"

"Throw names all you want. But if you're tempted to throw lead, I'd advise against it."

Glaring, Matt snarled, "You've just pulled down a whole mountain of trouble on yourself, Marshal."

Cash heard footsteps outside and sidled farther along the wall so he could cover everyone in the room as well as the entrance.

Sheriff Hain rushed in, his six-gun drawn, and quickly absorbed what had happened and then glanced at Cash. He holstered his weapon and lifted his hat, scratched his head. "Marshal, I reckon you best leave town. The Jacobson ranch hands are a tough bunch, and loyal."

"The fight was fair," Cash said.

"That's true, Sheriff," said the barkeep. "I was a witness."

Hain scowled at the bartender and strode over to the Jacobson brothers. He knelt on one knee beside Jerry.

"Alex has gone for the doc, Sheriff," Matt mumbled.

Hain shook his head and eyed Cash. "Jacobson won't let you get away with this, even if it was a fair fight."

"I'll stay, Sheriff. Grateful for your concern, though." Cash carefully moved to the entrance, gun in hand. He backed through the batwings and only then holstered his weapon after he'd turned the corner.

* * *

Judge Virgil McPiece opened the door as Cash mounted the steps to the porch. "Come in, I heard you were back in town." He thumbed at the saloon. "Sounds like you've been busy."

"I just gut shot Jerry Jacobson," Cash said as he entered and removed his hat.

Judge McPiece shut the door and led him along a short hall into a parlor. "That isn't good news. I suppose he had it coming?"

Cash nodded.

"Well, that won't cut any ice with Jacobson. He'll send his whole ranch after you, I reckon."

"If he does, he'll be breaking the law."

"Law's fragile enough already round here, Cash Laramie. It won't take much to break it for good."

"Maybe. That's not why I called on you, anyway. I wondered if anyone turned up to identify the two corpses on display."

The judge grinned. "Two people did—independently, I might add."

"And?"

"One of them was Ma Bartleby, the owner of the cathouse. Ash Devlin and Tiny Pucket frequented her place as customers a couple of times." He rooted inside a writing desk drawer and produced a telegram. "I wired Cheyenne and got a quick response—both are wanted in Ohio for bank robbery, rape and murder …"

"Why am I not surprised? You said two people."

"I did, didn't I? Our estimable printer Mr. Eldridge saw Tiny Pucket—he wasn't difficult to miss—entering the back door of the mayor's home the day before the attack on Mrs. Tolliver. Of course, he never thought anything about it, at the time."

"Will Eldridge testify?"

"I think so."

"Keep this quiet for now—if for no other reason than to protect Eldridge."

"I can do that. Until there's a prosecution case against our mayor, I don't have to divulge all."

Cash pulled out a sheet from his vest. "This is Wexler's confession—witnessed by Jane Maddison."

The judge quickly scanned the writing then looked up sharply. "This is pretty damning, Cash. Wexler makes no bones about it, the mayor hired him to kill Dean Tolliver."

"I know. Unfortunately, both Wexler and the witness to his confession are dead."

Slumping down in his chair, the judge let out a sigh of exasperation. "Damn … If it can be proved that Miss Maddison's signature is genuine, I believe it will still stand as evidence—damning evidence."

"That's what I wanted to hear, Judge."

"There's no way we can build a case against Brett Nolan before the election."

"But if you started proceedings, it's bound to harm his chances, isn't it?"

"Yes, I guess it would, at that. Before you turned up, I thought the mayoral election would be heated. Now, I fear it's going to hit the boiling point. God knows, I've tried to defuse the situation, but there are too many hotheads about."

He fingered his chin. "And I'll be seeing some of them at my bench, I warrant, before the two weeks are out."

"Well, either you or the undertaker," Cash replied.

CHAPTER 6

A Lawyer's Word

"It isn't often we get a marshal gracing my parlor," Ma Bartleby said, ushering Cash into the plush room. The place smelled of excess perfume, to hide the sweat and other odors the clients brought with them. He'd visited enough similar establishments in his time.

"I wanted to confirm that you'd appear as a witness concerning those two miscreants, Ash Devlin and Tiny Pucket," he said, removing his hat.

"And here I was thinking you fancied riding one of my girls!" She laughed and it came out a bit like the bray of a jackass. Her looks compensated, however, if you were partial to women with large breasts and purple eyes. As she laughed, her chest wobbled. And her eyes were alight with mischief and seemed to convey that she'd seen it all and was wise to every con known to man.

"I wouldn't say no, Mrs. Bartleby," he said, "once my business is concluded."

"That's what I like to hear. A man who knows his own mind! And call me Ma, everybody I like does."

"So, Mrs. ... Ma, will you vouch for the presence of Devlin and Pucket on the days specified?"

She nodded. "Oh, yes." She leaned close, her scent invading his nostrils so that he had to fight off an urge to sneeze. "It pleasured me a great deal to see those two bastards displayed outside Mr. Peel's emporium. They didn't treat my girls kindly, not at all."

"Thanks, Ma."

"Now then," she said, rubbing her hands together, "who shall I honor you with?"

Cash grinned. "I leave it in your hands."

At that, she guffawed. "I think not—let's put it in Rachel's. She's a lovely girl!"

Rachel was everything that Ma Bartleby promised—and more. She was bright and accomplished. Cash found that he could prolong his performance if he let his mind wander. It was tricky and didn't always work, but usually he was able to wallow in the pleasure and pace himself at the same time. In one of these interludes, he wondered about Esther and her crusade for women's right to vote. For sixteen years she'd had that particular bit between her teeth and now she was risking all—her life and even her son's.

He shook off thoughts about Danny's provenance and while he made love for the second time that night he thought about Lenora back in Cheyenne. Lenora was a puzzle for Esther, he reckoned. Lenora wasn't one of those whores in servitude; she'd actually chosen the profession. He'd asked her about that once, and she'd replied, "I get to meet a lot of real nice men." Then she'd shrugged. "And a lot of real bastards, as well. But the nice ones tend to make up for them. Otherwise, I wouldn't do it." He was ambivalent about her career choice. Sometimes, he felt jealous, yet at other times he dismissed it as "just a job."

And he had to admit that he wasn't faithful to Lenora in the physical sense—though his heart always seemed to belong to her, no matter what other woman he poked.

Right now, he lay back with a half-smoked cheroot, while Rachel dragged out smoke from her quirly. And he wondered how Lenora would vote, if she'd been given the chance.

He grinned, gripping the cigar between his teeth. Maybe a woman mayor would clamp down on loose living and whoring …?

"What's so funny, Marshal?" Rachel asked, stubbing out her cigarette in a bedside ashtray.

"Life, mainly."

* * *

It was in the early hours, before dawn, when the noise awoke him. Rachel was asleep, her arm draped across his chest. It was semi-dark and he could barely make out the room's furniture. Instinctively, before he'd even analyzed the sound, he reached for his holster draped on the bed-head and pulled out his Colt. In the same instant, a flaming bottle smashed against the wooden wall of the room, next to the door. The broken window glass had awoken him. Now, flickering flames lit up the room and created darting shadows.

His second impulse was to grab Rachel's arm and roll sideways, off the bed. Not a moment too soon. A spray of bullets peppered the wall and door.

Ricochets and bits of wood seemed to fly everywhere.

Then the gunfire stopped.

He heard shouts in the passage and more calls outside. He grabbed a sheet, beat the flames down, and smothered them.

When he turned up the oil lamp, he noticed that Rachel lay quite still on the floor by the bed. He rushed over and knelt beside her. Judging by the big bruise on her temple, she'd been knocked out when she hit the floor. A glancing splinter of wood had pierced her upper arm, otherwise she was unharmed and breathing. At least, he thought, this was one woman lady-killer Cash Laramie didn't get killed. And though she was an intimate stranger, he felt glad. Death was easy. He'd dealt it fairly and unfairly over the years. But sometimes, he didn't want to know about the innocent who died. Sure, Rachel was far from innocent—but she sure as hell didn't deserve to die just because she'd bedded him.

Ma Bartleby's voice resonated down the passage. Then Cash noticed something that hadn't been in the room earlier—a paper-wrapped stone, lodged against the base of the wardrobe. Maybe that had broken the window, not the flaming bottle.

He picked it up and removed the string that secured the paper. They'd meant to scare, not kill. The note didn't mince words: *Get the hell out of our town!*

* * *

Next morning, Cash sent an urgent cable to Cheyenne and hoped his request would be met. Then he mounted up and headed out to the Tolliver place. He felt confident that nothing had happened to Esther or Danny in his absence, since no word had reached town to that effect.

He was made welcome, and Esther opened the printer's parcel with glee, as if it contained a birthday present. When she smiled or laughed, it was as though the years dropped off her.

"These are just what I need, Cash. I want to start my campaign in town today," she said.

"That's fine by me. I'll accompany you." He eyed Danny. "What about you, son?"

"I'll stay here, protect our place." He thumbed at the Greener.

Briefly, Cash recalled all those years ago when he'd hidden in the barn loft with that same shotgun. He smiled and he was sure he caught Esther reminiscing the same night as well.

She stood up. "Let's git." She hugged Danny, kissed his cheek.

"Ma, that's enough—I'm grown, now!"

She smiled. "So you are … and I reckon young Ada knows that too."

He blushed. "Go on, Ma. Get your votes."

"Right. We've a lot of ground to cover with my leaflets."

They rode on into town.

With Cash by her side, Esther walked the length and breadth of the town, delivering leaflets by hand. Several shopkeepers were happy to stick her poster in their window. A few turned her down, however. "I guess I know already which way a good number of citizens will vote," she observed.

"Maybe," Cash said. "But just because Jameson the baker doesn't want your poster, it doesn't mean his wife's going to vote the same way as him."

Esther chuckled. "That's right! Wait 'til I give them an ear-banging tomorrow—the church hall's booked for my rally and I'm expecting a big crowd."

They rode under a banner that proclaimed *Brett Nolan brings prosperity to Bear Pines. Vote him in again!*

Esther bridled. "Prosperity for Mayor Nolan and his cronies, that's all!"

"Banners look impressive," Cash said. "But they don't sway minds."

"I suppose so. Well, we might get an idea who's backing me tomorrow."

* * *

That evening, at the end of their meal, Cash was alerted by the sound of riders approaching. He rose from the table and strapped on his gun-belt.

He peered out the window. "Six riders."

Esther peered over his shoulder. "They're Jacobson's men," she said. "Led by Matt." She rested a hand on his arm. "Stay here, for now. I'll go see what they want."

She unlatched the door and picked up the rifle that stood by the entrance. "Danny, get the Greener."

Danny was already carrying the shotgun to the far window on their left.

She nodded at both of them then opened the door and stepped onto the porch just as the riders drew rein.

"Good evening, Mrs. Tolliver," said Matt Jacobson. "Sorry to bother you, but we've come for Cash Laramie."

Esther stood with the rifle in the crook of her arm. "What do you want with a U.S. Marshal?"

"My brother died an hour ago. Laramie killed my brother—and he's going to pay."

"I'm sorry to hear your brother's dead, Matt Jacobson. But shouldn't a court decide who pays?" she asked, raising her rifle slightly.

"The law is what we make in these parts, lady. If you don't comply with our request, we're going to kill you and burn down your home."

"Comply? Seems like a lawyer's word, that—comply. Which stone did you find it under?"

"I advise the Jacobsons," said Mack Jenkins, the local attorney, urging his mount alongside Matt's. "And my advice to you, Mrs. Tolliver, is to comply with Mr. Matt Jacobson's request—or you will suffer the consequences."

She grinned and took a short step to the left, away from the door. "You know, Jenkins, this sounds a mite familiar."

"What do you mean?" Matt said.

"Some sixteen years ago, I faced down four men who had similar ideas about setting light to my home."

"Yeah," Matt said, "is that so?"

"What happened?" Jenkins asked.

"I did." Cash stepped out onto the porch, alongside Esther.

"It's him," Matt yelled. "Gun him down!"

"Drop your weapons!" barked an authoritative voice to their rear, before anyone could make a move.

Matt swiveled in his saddle. "Who the hell are you?"

Gideon Miles eased his grulla forward, his Winchester pointing at their backs. "The law, that's who."

"The hell you are!" snarled Matt. "You're a black—"

Miles shot Matt's hat off, then peeled back his smart pale gray jacket and revealed his U.S. Marshal's badge. "—and a good shot, as well."

"I'd do as he says," Cash advised, hand resting on his Colt.

Esther raised her Winchester and Danny's Greener poked out the window.

Two fools tried for their guns—and died, one shot by Miles, the other by Cash. Horses whinnied and backed off from the gunfire.

As the smoke cleared, the other four raised their arms.

"That's sensible of you," Cash said. "The odds were never on your side, Mr. Jacobson. Now, ease off those gun-belts—one at a time."

Obediently, the men unbuckled their belts and let them drop to the ground at their horses' feet.

"Ride over here to the hitch rail and dismount—again, one at a time." Cash gestured with his gun. "I don't want to get nervous 'cause of any sudden moves."

"You, nervous?" Miles said with a chuckle as he dismounted. "That'll be the day." He collected the gun-belts from the two dead men and from the ground where the others had been discarded.

While Cash tied the wrists of each man with piggin' string, Miles said, "Got your wire—seemed kinda urgent, so here I am, yet again plucking your fat out of the fire."

"Esther and I could've handled it," Cash said.

"And me," chipped in Danny from the window.

Appraising Esther as she rested her rifle against the wall, Miles grinned. "Well, I reckon you could, at that."

"But your intervention was helpful," Cash allowed.

Miles removed his hat and gave a slight bow. "Mrs. Tolliver, I presume?"

"Yes," she said, taking his big hand in hers. "Cash has told me a lot about you," she said, studying Miles' flamboyant clothes and shining black boots.

"Not everything, I hope?"

"I don't know everything about you, yet," Cash said. "You still spring surprises on me from time to time."

Miles grinned. "Makes life interesting, doesn't it?"

"It seems my life's like a Chinese curse already," Esther remarked.

"Just so," Miles said. "I suppose we'd better get these two bodies and our gun-happy gang back into town pronto."

"That should prove interesting too," Cash replied.

On their way, Miles observed, "Seems like the women in this territory have been freed from slavery, eh?"

"Slavery's one way of putting it, Mr. Miles," Esther said. "Drudgery still happens, though."

Cash gave Miles an odd look and he wondered again about Lenora. "Maybe all people will get to vote one day," he said.

Miles bit back, "Yeah, maybe in a hundred years!"

CHAPTER 7

Bullets for a Ballot

As the deputy named Zeke turned the key on the last of the cells, Sheriff Hain's face didn't reflect much pleasure. "This is a big mistake, Marshals—locking up three Jacobson men and young Matt."

"Well, we could've sent them all over to Mr. Peel, I guess," Cash said. "Would that have made you feel better?"

Hain grunted. "No, you getting the hell out would make me feel better. Nothing else."

"Hey, you didn't throw that message through Ma Bartleby's window, did you?"

Scowling, Hain snapped, "What the hell do you take me for?"

"A man the mayor's bought, Sheriff Hain. That's who."

The deputy let out a gasp and backed away from them.

Hain's face reddened and his jaw clenched. He seemed fit to burst, ready to spring at Cash, but his sense of self-preservation won. "You don't have to live here—sometimes, there's no choice but to …" He sighed. "What the hell, you'd never understand!" He turned on his heel and stormed out of the office.

From the sheriff's office window, Cash watched Hain stride angrily down the boardwalk until he was out of sight. "Where's he off to now?"

"Probably the mayor's," the deputy said.

"Figures," Miles said.

* * *

Next day, as Esther Tolliver approached the church hall for her talk, a crowd of quite vociferous townspeople met her. A young reporter from the *Pines Gazette*, pencil and pad in hand, asked the first question: "What have you got to say about these reports, ma'am?"

"Reports, what—?"

Someone thrust the morning *Gazette* under her nose.

Cash glimpsed the front-page headline: *Mrs. Tolliver's affair with a cowboy!*

"This is scurrilous nonsense," Esther snapped, "cooked up by the incumbent mayor. He's frightened he might lose, so he attempts to impugn my name."

"Have you any proof, ma'am?" the reporter asked.

"More to the point, has the newspaper editor?" she riposted.

"Well, not so as I've heard ..."

"*Exactly* my point!"

For a second, Cash reflected how Esther would have been hounded if their relationship had become public knowledge in Cheyenne sixteen years ago. It would have been much worse than this, he reckoned.

He and Miles eased people away to allow Esther to get to the doors.

"You know, I think you'll have a full hall," Cash said.

"Yes, but they're here for all the wrong reasons," she wailed.

"You've got a captive audience," Cash said, opening the door. All the seats were occupied; it was standing room only. "Use that and tell it straight."

As she mounted the steps to the small stage, there was muted applause, almost equaled by grumbling and general murmurs of discontent.

"I want to thank everyone for attending today," Esther began.

"Spill the dirt, Mrs. Tolliver!" shouted Jameson, the baker.

"I assure you, Mr. Jameson, although I work my land, I've been most careful not to track any honest dirt into this hall."

That got a few laughs.

"You know what I mean, woman—were you having an affair last year with that vagrant who called himself a cowboy?"

She let out a laugh. "I suppose the election was bound to turn dirty," she said, pointing at the baker. "I hope you've washed *your* hands."

That got a small laugh, so she went on, before Jameson could respond, "My husband was away on business. That 'vagrant cowboy' was actually my nephew, down on his luck. I gave him work for a week, paid him what he'd earned and he left. He slept in the barn. My son will vouch for it."

"He's your son, his word don't count," argued Jameson.

Nik Morton

"You're in the mayor's pocket, Mr. Jameson, so I shouldn't think that your word counts for much, especially since I know the mayor's promises are worthless."

Finally, she received an uproarious cheer, mainly from women.

"Now, young man," she said, addressing the reporter at the front, his pencil still poised over his pad, "if you'd be good enough to report the true words spoken in this gathering instead of gossip and claptrap, maybe we'll have an election we can believe in—for a change."

More cheers.

"Because that's what I'm here for, to advocate change. Change for the better. And for all the citizens of Bear Pines, not just those few in league with Brett Nolan."

The hall erupted. She'd converted the majority of her captive audience with just a few impassioned words, strongly felt and delivered. Cash felt proud of her.

And, he thought, since the mayor wants to throw mud, let's see if there's any dirt on Mr. Brett Nolan.

* * *

Miles and he agreed that at all times one of them would be with Esther during her politicking. Right now, it was Miles' turn to guard her. Cash took the opportunity to stroll through town. He called in at the various stores and made no apology for garnering support for Mrs. Tolliver as mayor. He also distributed fliers, urging the populace to vote for Mrs. T., as she was known by many.

He was surprised how many individuals were willing to speak up, providing nobody else was around. Within a few hours he'd built up quite a dossier of chicanery and favoritism spawned by Mayor Nolan.

The mayor bought several votes and purchased some businesses and properties from people who suddenly found that they had to leave town in a hurry. Usual excuse was, family trouble back east. As one voluble storekeeper stated, "Nothing can be proved, you know. But we tend to know who we can risk talking to, and our grapevine is pretty accurate."

Cash obtained two statements from men who were threatened on behalf of Nolan. "Sell up or lose everything," they'd been told.

Nolan owned a considerable spread abutting ranches that sold out. "It's no secret, Nolan wants to expand," said the shoe smith.

"Grab more land, that's what," snapped the man's wife. "He's a bandit!"

"Sure, we know, Alice, we know. But keep your voice down. The marshal can hear you without shouting. It's the folk in the street I don't want hearing you."

"I'm only telling it like it is," Alice went on. "Nolan's took the Sullivan place and he's already started building a mansion there 'cause it has the best views overlooking the valley."

"The Sullivans?" Cash queried.

"Oh, the Sullivans left hastily one night, without any farewells," the man explained. "Alice took it hard—they were our friends."

When dusk fell, Cash had finished his rounds for the day and carried four interesting documents, a damning indictment against the mayor, though he was no legal bird. He'd best leave them with the judge.

Cash emerged from the grocer's when he noticed the stark illumination down the end of the town. His mouth went very dry. No, surely not …

Judge McPiece's home was on fire, flames spouting out of both downstairs windows, on each side of the portico. Cash quickly scanned the gathered crowd and asked if anyone had seen the judge.

Nobody had. "I think he's still in there!" a distraught woman cried.

Without a moment's hesitation, Cash ran up the steps and into the hall. Flames licked the banister rail and climbed the stairs. Taking two steps at a time, he raced up, drawn by the judge's shouts. "Lisa, oh God, I can't manage!"

Cash reached the bedroom door. Curled in a fetal ball on a sheet on the floor was an elderly woman in a nightdress and standing beside her was the judge. There was a large cut on the judge's brow and he seemed to have a bloody shoulder. Yet he struggled manfully to haul his wife across the parquet flooring, tugging at the sheet under her. Then he collapsed to his knees.

Rushing in, Cash lent a hand and they hauled the woman out onto the landing. Cash grabbed Mrs. McPiece and swung her over his broad shoulder. "Quick, Judge—down the stairs—I'll bring your wife!"

Coughing on smoke, they emerged in the small front garden as behind them timbers groaned and collapsed noisily somewhere inside the building.

Many hands helped carry Mrs. McPiece to the Wordsworth Hotel, where a set of rooms was set aside for the judge and his wife.

The McPieces slept as soon as their heads hit the pillows. Cash stayed with them and, from the hotel room, he watched the house burn to the ground.

After a while, he felt a hand on his shoulder and started. He must have dozed.

Daylight slithered across the town and highlighted the black timbers. He turned.

"You sleep all right, Judge?"

"Surprisingly, considering what we've lost."

"It's the body's way of coping, I guess."

"Perhaps." The judge shook his head. "I'm afraid all the papers and law books have been burned. I hoped to get Lisa out first, then go back in for them."

"It's only paper."

"But there was that statement—with Miss Maddison's signature."

"It can't be helped."

"I think it could be helped, Marshal. It was deliberate." He lifted a hand to his bandaged head. "Somebody hit me while I sat at my desk in the study. When I came to, the fire was raging, already too severe. I rushed upstairs ..." He buried his head in his hands.

"How's your wife?"

"The doc fears she won't live out today. Too much smoke inhalation, he says." He paced up and down, balling his hands into fists, repeatedly. "To think, I'll only have this one day with her." He ground his teeth.

Cash crossed the floor and grasped the judge by his shoulders. "Then, go to her."

Nodding, the judge said, "Yes, yes, I must."

Cash picked up his two statements from the sideboard. "Don't get these burned. They might be useful."

Judge McPiece glanced at them. "These are very powerful arguments against Nolan. You've clearly a way of extracting information, Marshal."

"They divulged all that without duress, I assure you."

"And Wexler?"

"He was too stubborn for his own good. But his words were genuine enough."

"Yes." The judge clasped the papers to his chest. "I'll keep these safe, be assured. But what will you do?"

"I've a good mind to go out to the Jacobson ranch and mete out my own form of rough justice," Cash said, grimly.

The judge warned, "If you kill off too many folk, there'll be none left to make the vote worthwhile. Fear's spreading in the town. I can smell it. A lot of people are already thinking, better the devil you know ..."

Cash smiled. "I'm one devil they don't know. And I guarantee some of them are bound for hell."

* * *

"I think I can do this," she said on the first day. "But I still need your help, boys."

"I ain't been called a boy in a long while, ma'am," Miles said.

For the next few days, the routine was unvaried. Either Cash or Miles accompanied Esther into town while the other stayed at the ranch house with Danny. Esther glad-handed several voters and gave her speeches without hindrance.

She seemed to get considerable support and little heckling. Many townsfolk agreed with her view that Mayor Nolan employed too many dirty tricks. The fire at the judge's house—and his wife's death—seemed to strengthen their resolve, rather than weaken it.

Today, it was Miles' duty turn with her and he wondered if this was the way of things in the future. Word had it the territory wouldn't be long in joining the Union as a full-fledged state. Maybe, he thought, the way of the ballot would remove the way of the gun.

Mrs. Tolliver pointed down the alley adjacent to the saloon. "My husband's dearest wish was to serve this town and its people, to finally be rid of graft and favoritism. And he was gunned down by two men who were in the pay of the present mayor, Brett Nolan!"

There were gasps and exclamations of disbelief.

Miles watched her work the crowd. She seemed determined, fearless.

"Judge McPiece has proof, signed statements from the murderers of my husband!"

"Out with Mayor Nolan!" chanted a couple of women.

In a few seconds, the words were taken up by others. "Throw out the mayor. Mrs. Tolliver for mayor!"

She smiled and waved.

Several gunshots sounded in succession.

Miles felt the stabbing pain in the back of his shoulder as he spun round and landed on one knee. As he reached for his Colt, he saw Mrs. Tolliver drop to her knees, a hand clutching her left forearm. Blood trickled through her fingers.

The people in the crowd scattered in all directions, some shrieking, others wailing. At least two had also been shot.

Leaflets canvassing a vote for Mrs. Tolliver for mayor scattered like confetti, a few even splattered with blood.

CHAPTER 8
Stewed Vegetables

"Marshal," Danny said, shielding his eyes from the sun, "someone's riding hard. I reckon they're in a hurry."

Cash chambered a shell and stood in the shade of the veranda, waiting.

A minute or so later, Deputy Zeke McCain reined in by the porch. "Marshal, your friend Marshal Miles and Mrs. Tolliver have been shot! The sheriff said to come right away!"

"Ma!" wailed Danny, running down the steps and standing beside Zeke. "Is she all right?"

Zeke nodded. "Yes, it's only a flesh wound."

"And Marshal Miles?" Cash asked.

"Shot in the back, I heard."

"Danny," Cash said, "you stay here and watch the ranch house. I'll go into town with Zeke. Maybe I can find who bushwhacked your ma and Miles." He whistled for his horse, as he'd kept Paint saddled—just in case he was needed in a hurry—and let him graze in the shade behind the barn.

As he mounted, Cash said, "Don't let any Jacobson men anywhere near your home. Shoot to scare them off."

"Right, Marshal."

"I'll be back with your ma as soon as I can." He reined Paint around and rode off with Zeke.

Danny stood, pacing the porch for about ten minutes. Then he strode over to the well and ladled some water out of the bucket. Lukewarm, but it helped slake his thirst. It was damned hot.

Barely twenty minutes after Cash Laramie left, Danny noticed a small dust cloud approaching from the west. That sure wasn't the direction of the Jacobson spread. He narrowed his eyes and watched.

Two riders crested a nearby rise and rode on down to the entrance. "Hello, anyone there?" a woman called.

Danny stepped down from the porch and waved the Greener above his head. "Yo, I'm here—who is that?"

"It's Mrs. Nolan—come to talk to you and the marshal," she shouted.

He was about to say that the marshal wasn't here, but thought better of it. Best to find out what the mayor's wife wanted first. "Come in, Mrs. Nolan, and give your horses a drink—I'm sure they'll welcome it."

"Thanks," she called and spurred her horse ahead of the other man.

When she reached the horse trough to his right, she stepped down and led the animal to the water. She wore a split riding skirt, a green cotton shirt and a black hat. Her black leather boots were tooled with some kind of silvery filigree. She walked up to him and removed her gloves, held out her hand.

He shook—a light, quite soft hand—softer than Ma's. Close up, she was very attractive. He caught a whiff of some scent, sweet smelling, the kind of stuff Ma put on if there was a special event to attend.

Mrs. Nolan smiled. "Is the marshal here?"

"Not right now. What do you want, Ma'am?"

Her brow creased in concern as she said, "I just heard your mother was shot."

"Yeah, I know. Bad news travels fast."

The man moved his horse closer, next to Mrs. Nolan's.

"Well, son," she said, "I think things have gone too far. I'm fearful that my husband might get hurt as well. There are too many hotheads out there right now."

The man astride his mount nodded.

She went on, "I was hoping you or the marshal could speak to my husband and persuade him to step down."

Danny lowered the Greener. "I can't see the mayor listening to me, ma'am."

"I think he will," she said, "if I stand with you."

He grinned. This was too good an opportunity to miss. If they could talk to the mayor and convince him he didn't have the backing of the townsfolk, maybe Mr. Nolan would step down. "All right. Where is he—your husband?"

"Out at the Sullivan place."

"Yeah, I remember. You bought them out, didn't you?"

She nodded.

"Okay, I'll come with you."

"Good. I was hoping you would."

"I'll just get saddled up."

"We can wait, son." She smiled at him. "What's your name, again?"

101

"Daniel, ma'am. Danny."

"Well, Danny, I think we'll make a good team." She took his hand again and shook it. Her eyes seemed only for him.

He flushed and reluctantly let go of her hand. "Yes, ma'am. I won't be long."

* * *

When Cash rode in, Sheriff Hain seemed to have covered everything. The shooter—there'd definitely only been the one—had fired on the group, rather than at anyone in particular. "He was on horseback, waiting," said Hain. "Down that same damned alley, in the shadows. He just let rip and then rode out the other end of the alley, left town before anyone had a chance to realize what was happening."

"Send anyone after him?" Cash asked.

"Sure, I sent Burt. He may be young, but he's good."

"Okay. I'll be over at the doc's if you have any news."

"Sure, Marshal. Don't worry, we'll get the bastard, whoever he is."

Cash turned on his heel and strode toward the doctor's surgery and home. On his way, he wondered about the sheriff. Hain seemed genuinely surprised and annoyed about the shooting. Maybe it had nothing to do with the mayor? Unless the sheriff wasn't in on it.

The doctor's office closely resembled the field hospitals he'd heard about. There were four townsmen sitting or lying around, while the nurse moved from one to the other, bandaging as she went. Cash spotted Miles, who lay on his front on a bloodstained table.

Miles waved and grimaced. "At least it was my left shoulder—shouldn't affect my gun-hand one bit."

"What happened?"

"Ambush—straight after Mrs. T. told the crowd the mayor had paid for her husband to be murdered."

Cash glanced around. "Where is she?"

Miles shrugged and nodded at a door at the side of the room. It was labeled *Private*. "Probably in the back—I heard another woman was shot, too. Nothing serious. I suppose they're keeping us separate."

Cash nodded. "I won't be long. I just want a word with the doctor."

"Sure. I ain't going anywhere."

Cash walked over to the door, knocked and opened it.

The doctor extracted a .22 bullet from a woman's abdomen. A nurse hovered over the woman who was unconscious, only the midriff exposed. "What do you want, Marshal?" the doctor asked gruffly. "You can see, I'm rather busy."

"I'm looking for Mrs. Tolliver."

"She isn't here."

"I heard she caught the stage," the nurse said. "It left not ten minutes after the shooting."

"Maybe that's the most sensible thing that woman's done," the doctor said. "Quit the town."

The nurse gave him a withering look but refrained from responding.

Cash turned to the nurse and whispered, "Where does the stage stop over next?"

She shrugged. "Can't say I know, Marshal. Try the depot—they'll tell you."

"Thanks, ma'am. Doc," he said and left.

* * *

At the stage depot, Cash questioned the owner, a wiry bald-headed man. "Did you see Mrs. Tolliver get on the stage?"

"Sure did. Poor woman," he said. "We sure don't deserve her, I can tell you. No wonder she quit."

Cash frowned. He knew her and there was no way she'd up and leave. "Where's the stage headed?"

"Fort Bridger."

But that wasn't anywhere near her ranch house. What about Danny? She wouldn't leave without her son. "Did you definitely see her get on the stage?"

"Sure did. She seemed to have difficulty boarding. A bearded man with a limp and a purple bandana helped her up. She sure didn't look too well. White as a sheet."

He knew the answer, but had to ask the question anyway. "Was Mrs. Tolliver's son with her?"

"Nope. Just them two boarded." The man shuffled some papers. "If that shooting had happened maybe an hour or so earlier, I'd have bet a few more might have wanted to catch the stage out of this damned town."

* * *

"Excuse me, Mrs. Nolan, but this isn't the way to the Sullivan place," Danny said.

"No, you're right. I was mistaken. It's your mother who's going there—not you."

"Pardon?"

She smiled. "I can see you're confused." She gestured to the taciturn rider alongside them. "Craig, please enlighten him.

"Sure, ma'am." Craig Bond whipped out his pistol and slammed the butt on the back of Danny's head.

The boy slumped in his saddle and Angelina Nolan swiftly reached out a hand and steadied him. She reined in her horse and Danny's stopped too. "Tie him to his saddle for now."

"You sure this is part of the plan, ma'am?" Craig asked.

"Yes, of course. You and Felix will soon get your own back on Mrs. Tolliver—or Traynor, as you knew her."

"Whatever it takes," Craig said, dismounting. "We've both waited a long time for this."

"Just so," she said, nodding. She withdrew a Derringer from her skirt pocket and covered the unconscious boy, just in case.

Once Danny was tethered to his saddle, they set out for the Nolan ranch. It was less than an hour's ride.

"Where is everybody?" Craig asked, when they arrived.

"In town, listening to my husband. He needs their numbers to impress the townsfolk, I believe."

"Okay. Where do you want the boy?"

She pointed to a raised mound of earth with a door let into it, just on the right of the ranch house. "The root cellar should be ideal, I think."

They rode over and dismounted. Craig walked with a peculiar gait, toes pointing in. Angelina Nolan produced a key from her skirt pocket, shoved it into the root cellar door's padlock. She opened the door and was met by the smell of dried earth. "Throw him in there—let him stew for a while."

"Stewed vegetables—can't beat it on a winter's night," Craig said.

"Very witty." She stood, arms akimbo and watched as Craig sliced the rope binding Danny, unhorsed the boy and literally threw him through the doorway. The boy's body tumbled noisily down the dozen earth and wood stairs and then made a dull thudding noise.

"Good." She shut the padlock and turned to Craig. "You know what to do—go and welcome his mother."

As he mounted his horse, he grinned. "I've been looking forward to this for a long time."

"Yes, and you can wait a while longer." She raised a hand. "We agreed, remember, nothing is to happen to her until the election's over. She must be missing, not dead." She neglected to add that her husband knew nothing about any of this.

"Who said anything about killing her—yet?"

She was strangely aroused at the implication. While she was pleased she'd stumbled on this pair—Bond and Penny—and employed them with alacrity, she didn't particularly like Penny. And while Bond seemed too sure of himself, yet he held a fascination for her. She suspected that he might be a man of similar appetites to hers. The scar over his left eyebrow seemed to redden whenever he talked about violence. And that observation warmed her. Yet for now, she had to ensure that Mrs. Tolliver was unharmed until after the election—otherwise, Brett would lose. Brett's earlier attempts at getting rid of the Tolliver woman had been misguided and stupid. Sometimes, most times, Brett showed no subtlety. She smiled.

"You won't be long, I assume?" Craig said, turning his horse round.

"No, I have a few loose ends to tie up, then I'll join you both."

Craig fingered his hat brim at her and rode off.

She waited until the man was a speck on the horizon, then thrust the key in the padlock and opened the door. She pawed around on the right of the entrance and located an oil lamp. She lit it and adjusted the flame. The cellar smelled of damp earth and a variety of vegetables. The light illuminated the dark walls as she descended the wood treads laid out on earth steps.

The root cellar was quite large and allowed her to stand upright. Over on the right was a bed, complete with mattress. She and Jerry had enjoyed several earthy moments on there. She smiled for a fleeting instant then her heart felt pierced with agony. Those days of pleasure were gone, for good. Jerry was dead.

She found the boy slumped at the base of the steps. He supported himself on one elbow while he fingered his head. His eyes screwed up at the light of the lantern. "Where am I?" he queried, his voice weak and a little fearful.

She smiled. Maybe there was still pleasure to be had down here, after all. "You're in heaven, boy."

"Heaven?"

She bent down and grasped his arm and shoulder. "Here, let me help you to this bed."

As she led him across the earthen floor, he said, "It's dark and smells odd—what happened?"

It wouldn't take him long for his memory to return. "Just rest, you've had an awful accident," she soothed. "Here, lie down."

When he was lying on the grubby mattress, she deftly produced rope and gently secured one of Danny's wrists to the bedpost. She was fastening the other before he realized what was happening.

"What are you doing? Mrs. Nolan, is it?"

She stepped back and smiled. "Yes, it is. It seems your memory's coming back."

He nodded, alarm in his eyes. He attempted to pull his arms free, but she'd tied his wrists tightly. He kicked and writhed, but he couldn't get off the bed.

She grabbed a pillow and covered his face with it. Danny frantically struggled, shaking and shoving, bucking against her. She felt quite aroused as he fought for breath, for life.

As he grew less agitated, she raised the pillow. He was still breathing.

Now, she removed his boots and tied his ankles to the base of the bedstead. He was spread-eagled and helpless.

She drew the knife from her belt.

CHAPTER 9
Bad Penny

When Cash stepped out of the stage depot, he heard the mayor haranguing the people. "Mrs. Tolliver hasn't the backbone to be mayor," he said. He laughed and pointed at the end of the town's main street. "She caught the stage and hightailed it, instead of fighting for her beliefs."

But a handful of hecklers accused him of having done away with her.

"You're playing dirty, Nolan!"

"We all know you play with a marked deck!"

"If your people have hurt her, you'll be sorry!"

Nolan raised both hands, as if to show that he wasn't carrying any weapons or a marked pack of cards. "I must say, I'm mighty miffed at this false accusation!"

Cash suspected that Nolan was a good actor—he had to be to manipulate the townspeople for so long. But he didn't seem to be acting now. He realized that Nolan didn't need to do away with Esther. All he had to do was hold her somewhere until the voting was over. When she eventually turned up, he'd plead complete innocence and blame someone, anyone else.

Leaving Nolan to get a well-deserved drubbing from several voters, Cash crossed the road. At that moment, Burt the deputy rode in.

Cash stopped outside the sheriff's office. "Any luck, Burt?"

Burt shook his head. "Sorry, Marshal, but the bastard covered his tracks well."

"That's a shame." He gestured toward the doctor's surgery. "I'm calling in on the doctor. If you or Zeke have any information, let me know."

"Sure thing, Marshal."

Cash entered the doctor's surgery as Miles shrugged into a fresh white shirt. His wound was bandaged, and his smart jacket was slung over a chair with his gun-belt. "About time you came to get me out of here," Miles said.

"You're fit to travel, then?"

"Sure. Why?"

"We need to track the last stage out of town—Esther's on it."

Buttoning his jacket, Miles frowned. "I find it hard to believe that she'd up and quit, even if she was wounded."

"My thoughts precisely."

They rode out of town and along the stagecoach trail. The recent ruts were clear for a good way. Then, after about five miles of easy riding, there was a cluster of horse tracks, and the pronounced indentation of the stage wheels suggested that the coach had stopped for a while.

Four horse tracks moved northwest, away from the trail. In the direction of the old Sullivan place.

* * *

"Please, Mrs. Nolan, don't do this!" Danny's naked body writhed and squirmed on the bed, but he couldn't break the tethers. The shreds of his clothing lay scattered on the rough earth.

"What are you doing?" he demanded as she discarded her shirt.

"I'm going to ride you, boy, 'til your eyes pop!"

"No, I want to be pure for Ada—please don't do this," he pleaded.

"Pure?" She laughed, and slipped out of her chemise. The lambent glow of the lamp highlighted her contours and emphasized the dark areolas of her breasts. "That's not how I see you from here, boy." She unbuckled her belt.

"Why are you doing this?"

She dropped her skirt to the floor then paused, her attractive features suddenly twisted into a hideous grimace. "Why? Because your mother's pet marshal killed my beau, that's why."

"Your—your beau? But you're married."

She let out a high-pitched laugh. "One day you'll understand, boy. Marriage ain't what it's cracked up to be. It's all about power and need." She hurriedly removed the rest of her garments and, completely naked save for her boots, moved toward him. "And I need you—now!"

* * *

From the rise overlooking the cleared area, it was obvious that the new Nolan mansion was half-finished, but there were no workmen present now. "He works fast, don't he?" Miles said.

"The mayor has plenty of money, it seems," Cash said. "But is it his—or the town's?"

"There lies the rub," opined Miles. Then he pointed to two horses tethered at the corral to the right of the building. "Two shouldn't be difficult, I reckon."

"Let's take it easy. If she's seen their faces, they might feel inclined to kill her as soon as we show up."

Tying their horses to branches, they split up, left and right and descended the treed slope.

The only complete building was the bunkhouse—perhaps the builders stayed there overnight, Cash mused. He approached the corner at an oblique angle, so anyone at the windows wouldn't see him.

Miles moved slower than normal and headed for the mansion itself; from there he'd have a commanding view of the entrance to the bunkhouse and surrounding hardpan.

Cash reached the clapboard walls and hugged his back to them. His hand felt sweaty as he gripped the Colt. He heard voices—two men. May be more, though.

"The boss should be here soon with Craig," said one of them.

Cash's memory stirred, but he couldn't place the voice.

Could still be harmless workmen.

The other one spoke: "Do you reckon he's got a hankering after her, Felix?"

Felix? Vaguely familiar, but he couldn't snag the memory.

"Nah," said Felix, "she's too bossy for his taste."

"You're making a big mistake," said Esther, "keeping me here."

Not harmless workmen, after all.

Felix … Felix Penny? Was it twenty years since he was sent to prison? No, it wasn't. Maybe he got out for good behavior. Or escaped.

Then that meant the Craig he referred to was Bond, Craig Bond.

Figures, he thought. They probably wanted to get even with Esther and what better way than to sabotage her campaign for mayor. But would it simply end with her losing—or had Craig a more sinister kind of revenge on his mind?

He removed his hat and risked a glance through the bottom corner of the nearest window.

Felix Penny was recognizable, even though he now sported a black beard sprinkled with gray. He limped across the room toward Esther. She was secured to a straight-backed chair with a length of lariat. She seemed disheveled but otherwise unharmed. Her wounded left arm was bandaged with a purple bandana.

The other man lounged against the wall, loading and reloading his six-gun. "I think we can't let her live," he said.

"Don't do the thinking, Alec. Leave that to Craig."

"But she's seen our faces."

"Leave it. She stays alive 'til the end of the election. Craig says that's what his orders were—they don't want her body turning up before the election."

He'd heard enough.

Cash signaled to Miles.

Seconds later, Miles fired his rifle at the door, head-high.

As Felix and his pal Alec withdrew their pistols and turned, distracted, Cash fired through the window, shooting both in the back. They staggered against the wall.

Felix spun round, aimed at Esther. Cash drilled his forehead and he collapsed. Alec sat in a crumpled heap, whimpering, wheezing on a damaged lung.

Cash ran round to the door and kicked it in. Miles was right behind him as he entered.

Esther's eyes widened, pleased and surprised. "Cash—they've got Danny!"

"Here?" he asked, using his knife on her bonds.

"No, I don't think so." She shrugged off the severed lengths of rope and winced at the pain of her wound. "The man named Felix told me."

Cash nodded. "That's the only way you'd let them get you on that stage, isn't it?"

"Yes. They threatened to kill him if I didn't go along with them."

"You have no idea where Danny might be?"

"No ..." Her voice cracked.

Cash went over to the man with the bubbling lung. He knelt down. "Alec, is that your name?"

The man nodded, his eyelids heavy, drooping. "Yes," he croaked.

"Do you know where they took the boy?"

Alec's eyes glazed over, staring. Fear hovered there. His lower lip trembled. Cash unfastened the man's bandana and pressed it over the bubbling chest wound. For a second or two, Alec's breathing seemed quieter.

"I was only paid to watch her," Alec wheezed. "Felix didn't tell me much else."

Cash stood up. "He's not much use."

"Well, he's even less now," Miles remarked, pointing.

Alec was dead.

Esther gripped Cash's hand. "How are we going to find Danny?"

He hugged her and she cried against his chest. "We'll find him. I promise."

"I don't even know if he's still alive," she sobbed.

Those words cut into Cash like a knife, yet he couldn't account for his pained reaction. He'd known young men who met untimely and unfair deaths before. Why did the thought of Danny's death affect him?

* * *

Abused and corrupted at the age of twelve, Angelina learned the harshest lesson of life: you had to be strong and ruthless to get what you wanted. Now, she relished inflicting pain on the weak and the defenseless. And she derived much pleasure from corrupting the innocent.

Sated for the moment, she buttoned up her shirt and turned to the doorway of the root cellar. She left the oil lamp to burn low.

As she climbed the steps, she reflected that Brett never could understand her urges. Jerry was beginning to—until that damned marshal shot him.

She swung the door wide and the intense sunlight made her squint. Craig would be waiting. Maybe he'd replace Jerry in her affections? He had a hard edge to him—and a fierce grudge against Mrs. Tolliver.

Mrs. Tolliver. Just thinking of that woman brought a sly smile to Angelina's mouth. If only Mrs. Tolliver knew.

Her smile froze as Brett snapped, "What the hell are you doing down there?"

He strode from their ranch house porch, his smart black jacket dust-covered. He must have just ridden here from his rally in town.

She absently slammed shut the door, snapped the padlock. "Just checking on our provisions."

"Since when have you been interested in our vegetables?"

She shrugged. "Since I realized I'd married one?"

He raised a hand, about to slap her, then thought better of it. "You'd like me to, wouldn't you, you bitch?"

"Slap me, my dear, and I'll do much worse to you." She eyed his crotch meaningfully. "That is, if there's anything worth bothering with there."

"You used to enjoy it."

"I only pretended, you fool!" She brushed past him and made her way to her horse that stood patiently waiting.

She mounted and gazed down at her husband. Tears glistened, brimming in his eyes. He was weak, too—but he'd been useful to further her ambition, so she'd refrained from breaking him. He might still get into the state legislature, if he greased the right palms. And she'd ride on his coattails.

She leaned down, ran a hand over his face and used a thumb to brush away the moisture at his eyes. "Sorry, my dear. I'll make it up to you after the election. I promise." She blew him a kiss and rode off for her appointment with Craig Bond.

* * *

Craig halted his horse on the rise overlooking the Sullivan ranch. He watched as the two marshals rode out with the widow Traynor—or Tolliver. She seemed to collect dead husbands, he mused.

He ground his teeth together. It was tempting, to sit here and shoot them with his rifle. But he wasn't that good a marksman. In his day, Dan Fleming had been an exceptional shot—until that hay bail brained him. He was still in prison, happy to stay there, his mind no clearer after all these years had passed.

No, he thought, I'll have to bide my time.

For now, he'd better get back to Mrs. Nolan and tell her their plan had a severe hole in it.

Even so, they still had the boy. Yes, the kid was a good bargaining chip.

* * *

On their way to the Tolliver ranch, Cash said, "Did you recognize the guy named Felix?"

"No." She thought for a moment and then gasped, "Not Felix Penny?"

"The same. That limp, he got it from me, if you recall."

"He came to get even with me, is that it?"

"Could be. It's also likely that Craig Bond and Dan Fleming aren't too far away, either."

"Oh, my God—you mean they could be the men who took Danny?"

Cash nodded. "It's highly likely."

"What do we do now?"

"Check on your ranch. See if we can pick up their tracks."

At that moment, Miles reined in and indicated three coyotes fighting over a carcass in a slight depression on their right. A black cloud of flies hovered. "I thought I saw some blue—clothing, maybe," he said.

Cash fired a warning shot and the coyotes scurried off.

All three rode up and then Esther turned away and dry-heaved.

It was the remains of a man's torso.

Miles glanced around at more disturbed ground in the depression. "Over there," he pointed, and then added, "and over there, too."

Cash and Miles dismounted. It didn't take long to discover the three graves; wild animals had disturbed all of them and now flies buzzed. But there was no sign of a cross, headstone or other marker.

Esther rode up to the second grave as Cash scooped earth away from the head.

"Oh, God," she whispered, raising a hand to her mouth. "That's Mike Sullivan. He had a wife and a son."

"That explains the other two graves, I reckon," Miles said.

"I guess they didn't sell out, after all," Cash added.

* * *

Angelina Nolan strode into the sheriff's office. The eyes of the two young deputies widened and it seemed as though they had trouble keeping their tongues from lolling from their open mouths.

"Is the sheriff in?" she asked.

Sheriff Hain emerged from the back room. He doffed his hat, briefly. "What can I do for you, Mrs. Nolan?" Concern flashed across his face. "Nothing troubling the mayor, I hope?"

She smiled. "No, he's just fine. Looking forward to the election tomorrow, of course."

"Yes. He's bound to win."

The two deputies kept silent on the topic, their eyes never leaving her figure.

"Can you step outside, Sheriff? I have a favor to ask of you."

"Sure." He turned to his deputies. "Hold the fort 'til I get back, Zeke."

"Sure thing, Sheriff."

Hain stepped outside behind Mr. Nolan. He shut the door behind them, and they took a few paces along the boardwalk.

"What's the favor, Mrs. Nolan?"

"It's worth a great deal of money, if you're interested."

"I might be. What does it entail?"

Craig Bond stepped out from the nearby alley. "Sheriff, I'd like you to join me on a little hunting trip."

* * *

The discovery of the Sullivans changed their plans. They recovered the bodies as best as they could, then built a cairn of rocks that would be spotted easily enough. Cash said, "We've got to report this—and arrange for their reburial." Cash eyed the darkening sky, the gray clouds skimming the horizon. "Besides, it's getting late."

Esther reluctantly agreed, so they headed to town.

119

As they approached the entrance to Bear Pines, they rode past the cemetery. The backdrop of the coming sunset created a somber sight. The judge was burying his wife. It seemed as if most of the township had come to the funeral.

Esther cried, but Cash suspected it wasn't just about the judge's loss. She must be anxious to get on the trail of Danny's abductors.

"We need something to eat," Miles said as they dismounted in front of the sheriff's office.

Esther shook her head. "I couldn't eat a thing. If I did, I'd have trouble keeping it down."

"Howdy, Marshal," said Zeke, stepping out of the office. "Sheriff ain't in. Can I help?"

"You might want to send Mr. Peel out to the Sullivan place—there are two dead bodies in the bunkhouse."

Zeke grinned. "Your handiwork, Marshal?"

"Felons who committed the crime of kidnapping."

"I guess you don't take prisoners, eh, Marshal?"

"Sometimes, they don't want to come quietly. So, they get an eternity of quiet, instead."

Zeke chuckled then, raising his hat, added, "Glad to see you've come back, Mrs. Tolliver."

"Thank you, Zeke," she answered tremulously. "Good to be back."

Cash didn't want to mention the Sullivan bodies yet, until he'd spoken to the judge. Zeke had enough on his plate, as it was. "We'll be at the hotel—if Sheriff Hain returns," he said.

They were served steak, potatoes and peas in the hotel restaurant. Esther picked at her food, but was able to force a little down. Lines of worry creased her forehead. The election was tomorrow and Cash knew that she had no stomach for it while Danny was missing.

"We'll find him," he promised. "First light, we'll leave."

She gave a desultorily nod.

The judge joined their table shortly after they'd finished and were smoking cheroots. His face was sad and his shoulders were slumped. Cash gave him a cigar and then, briefly, explained what they'd found in the depression. "Would you be able to get the names of all those who've sold out to Nolan?" he asked.

The judge blanched. "You mean, there may be more?"

Cash blew smoke. "I'd bet on it."

* * *

As Cash promised, they were up at first light and set out for the Tolliver ranch. At Cash's insistence, they approached the ranch house with caution, but there was nobody waiting for them. There was no sign of any struggle, either, which heartened Esther. "Danny might have been lured away," she said, hope in her voice.

"Could be. He'd stand a better chance if he went along peaceably."

"But ... what that man said, about seeing their faces ..."

"I know. Let's hope we find them before that happens."

Miles identified the tracks. "Three horses—one from the barn."

"That would be Danny's—they rode out with him on his own horse."

Miles said, "Sounds hopeful."

* * *

Hope rose another notch when they spotted a rider approaching. It was Angelina Nolan and she seemed distressed. "Oh, Marshal Laramie, I'm glad I've caught up with you! I thought I might have to go right into town for the sheriff."

"The sheriff ain't there, ma'am. What's the matter?" Miles inquired.

She looked at Esther and let out a sigh. Her cheeks were flushed, her lips painted a deep strawberry red. "I'm sorry, Mrs. Tolliver, but I think my husband has gone berserk. He's kidnapped your son!"

"Where are they?" Cash demanded before Esther could respond.

"I'll take you—it isn't far."

"Okay—lead on, ma'am. But be careful."

Careful was the watchword, all right. Cash couldn't quite square Mrs. Nolan being so helpful that she was willing to thwart her husband's plans. He exchanged a wary glance with Miles, who winked.

About a mile down the trail, the road entered a steep-sided gully that seemed to have a dogleg halfway along.

Cash reined in and turned to Mrs. Nolan, raised an eyebrow.

She pointed, her fingernail tinted red. "They're holding young Danny in a shack on the other end of this gully."

Esther let out a faint gasp of concern.

"You two ladies wait here," Cash said. "We're going to investigate."

Esther said, "Be careful."

Nodding at the two women, Cash and Miles turned their mounts to the gully. Within seconds, they both urged their horses to greater speed, racing through the gully entrance. As they approached the dogleg, both drew their Colt revolvers.

Then they were out of sight.

A number of gunshots blasted out, echoing.

"That's a lot of gunfire," Angelina observed, a frown on her brow.

"Oh, God, I hope Danny's all right," Esther said, eyes fixed on the entrance.

At that moment, Angelina Nolan pulled out her rifle and slammed the butt to the side of Esther's head. Esther slumped forward then fell off her horse.

Angelina reined her mount around and rode back the way they'd come.

CHAPTER 10

Different Kind of Lawman

Expecting an ambush, Cash and Miles slid a foot out of their stirrups and clung to their horses' necks. Rifle fire cascaded to the gully floor, but the targets were moving too fast and were mostly hidden by their running horses.

Reaching a cluster of boulders at the roadside, Cash dropped from his horse, hit the ground and rolled under cover.

A few yards further up, Miles did the same. Their horses kept on running, away from the gunfire.

Bullets whanged off the rocks.

"Two of them," Cash called.

"Yep. Got one—over to my right."

"You're welcome to him. I'll take this one."

The ambusher above Cash fired down at the boulders, knocking chips of rock everywhere. Dust and smoke filled his nostrils. He lunged to a shaded section, behind more rocks. The ambushers probably didn't expect us to get so far through the gully, he thought.

Cash removed his boots and gun-belt. He'd have liked to slip on his moccasins, but they were in his saddlebag. Barefoot, with lithe quick movements, he scaled the higgledy-piggledy mass of outcropping rocks. He was silent, almost like a ghost. He carried his revolver in his hand and a knife in its sheath on his belt.

It sounded as though Miles was trading shots with the other ambusher. Maybe he was pinned down. He had to hope his friend would manage. He wasn't going to offer aid, as that would give away his position.

It took him perhaps ten minutes to negotiate the rugged side of the gully. The shooter had been obliging, advertising his whereabouts with random if ineffectual shots.

Now, the ambusher stopped firing, probably because Cash hadn't returned any shots for several minutes, in fact since he began his climb.

It didn't matter. Cash spotted him—just over to his right, about two yards below. As he'd intended, Cash had circled the man and gained an advantage above him.

He recognized the shooter. Definitely Craig Bond.

* * *

Miles fired and reloaded, pinning down the shooter, which was no mean achievement with only a Colt against a rifle. But Miles was a crack shot and evidently the ambusher wasn't.

He noted that the shooting over by Cash had stopped.

Time for a little ruse, he reckoned.

Miles took off his hat and tentatively held it out to his left, as far as he could reach, letting its crown jut above the line of rocks.

Bullets rained down, gouging out the rock, but missed the hat. The guy was a lousy shot. But even a badly aimed bullet could kill. Miles flicked the hat in the air, suggesting perhaps that its owner had been hit and at the same time he rolled to his right and stood, hammer cocked.

Sheriff Hain stepped out from one side of a big boulder, his rifle raised, ready, his mouth curved in a grin.

The grin froze as Hain noted Miles standing below to his left.

Miles extended his arm and fired as Hain brought his rifle round.

Hain dropped his weapon and clutched at his throat. The gargling sound he made seemed to fill the gully. The sheriff fell facedown among the scattered boulders.

"I reckon Zeke'll be the new sheriff now," Miles said.

* * *

Soundlessly, Cash jumped from his vantage point, landing directly behind Craig. His bare feet thudded into Craig's back and before Craig could react, Cash slammed his gun barrel against the man's temple. Craig dropped like a felled tree.

When Craig recovered consciousness, he found himself staked out and spread-eagled on the gully floor. His pants had been cut away and his legs and groin were bare. A pile of dried wood was clustered around his midriff and between his legs.

Nursing her sore head, Esther watched dispassionately from horseback. The bruise on her temple showed livid purple. To one side, Miles leaned against a boulder.

"I hope you appreciate the effort we've put into this," Cash told Craig. "Getting just the right kind of wood isn't easy in this place. It has to be tinder dry and not too big." He flicked a match, lit a cheroot.

"What the hell are you doing?"

"I'm doing the questioning, Craig." He puffed out smoke and extinguished the match, threw it onto the kindling between Craig's legs. Craig flinched. "You do the answering. That's how it works."

"Don't be stupid! I've got nothing to say."

"I think you have. You can start by telling us where you put young Danny. His ma's kinda anxious to locate him." He thumbed at Esther.

"You're a lawman," Craig said. "You aren't allowed to torture me."

"Cash is a different kind of lawman," Miles observed, filing a nail. "And I assure you, he's quite serious."

"Anyway," Cash said, "who said anything about torture?"

Craig craned his neck round. "Mrs. Tray—Tolliver, you can't let him do this!"

She closed her eyes briefly and shuddered, then opened them and looked daggers at him, but she didn't—or couldn't—speak.

Cash said. "I'm just asking a few questions, is all." He struck another match and flung it at the wood on Craig's torso.

Craig let out a squeal. The tinder quickly caught alight, and flames soon flickered.

"Oops, careless of me," Cash said.

"Put it out," Craig screamed, "quick!"

"What?" Cash said, raising a foot above the fire and Craig's groin. "Stomp it out?"

"Whatever, do it now!" He writhed and tugged at his tethers. "Please!"

Cash lowered his boot on the flaming tinder and smothered it with his sole, pressing down hard with his heel digging into the man's groin.

Craig groaned and hissed through his teeth. Sweat covered his entire face.

"You'd better start talking," Cash advised, "else I might have another accident with my matches…"

"Okay, okay—we took him to the Nolan's spread…"

"We've already been there—the building site's deserted," said Miles. "Try again."

Esther eased her mount closer, attentive. "Go on," she said coldly.

Cash lit another match.

"No!" Craig shrieked, "I meant the Nolans' ranch house. Where they live now. They won't move to the Sullivan place 'til it's finished."

"You'd better show us," Cash said and blew out the match.

* * *

Craig explained that they'd been able to buy the sheriff easily enough. Hain wanted to get out, before Nolan ruined everything he'd worked for, and this payoff answered his prayers. "Of course, now he ain't praying, he's with the angels."

"Devils, more like," said Esther.

Craig's hands were tied behind his back and his feet were tethered to the stirrups. He sat uncomfortably, bare-assed. Esther rode alongside, Winchester in the crook of her arm, constantly watching him.

They entered the Nolan spread and rode toward the root cellar.

"I put him in there," Craig said.

At that moment, the mayor strode down his porch steps, a Greener leveled threateningly. "Marshal, what are you doing on my property?" he challenged.

Cash dismounted. "Don't threaten an officer of the law, Mayor. It might prove fatal."

"Answer my question, damn you!" He raised the shotgun butt to his shoulder.

Cash drew his Colt and fired, just once, his bullet slicing into the mayor's left shoulder.

Mayor Nolan stumbled backward and dropped the weapon. He hissed between clenched teeth, a hand covering the wound.

Esther cocked her rifle and prodded Craig in the back. "Don't think about moving," she warned between gritted teeth.

"Keep your shirt on," Craig said, "I ain't going anywhere."

"Maybe to Hell," she said in a harsh whisper.

"Stay there, Mayor," Miles advised, "if you know what's good for you." He covered the mayor with his Colt.

Trembling with shock, the mayor docilely watched.

Cash walked up to the root cellar. He shot off the padlock and swung open the door. "Danny?" he called down into the musty darkness.

Then he walked inside, into the flickering dusky light.

* * *

A few seconds later, Cash came out and called to Miles, "Bring my bedroll." His voice sounded hollow. He stood, waiting, his eyes avoiding Esther's.

She sat astride her horse, clearly anxious, her rifle aimed at Craig.

Keeping an eye on the mayor, Miles walked over and handed Cash the bedroll. "Do you want me to come down with you?"

Cash shook his head. "No. I'll be up directly." He turned and re-entered the root cellar.

True to his word, he was back within a half-minute. In his arms he carried Danny, wrapped in the bedroll. A bare bloodstained forearm dangled loose.

Esther groaned. "Oh, my son!" Hastily, she dismounted and, still clutching the rifle, ran over.

"He's dead, Esther," Cash said, his voice dull. "I'm sorry, we were too late." Gently, he lowered Danny down on the warm earth under the sun's glare. He knelt beside the boy, unwilling or unable to rise.

The boy's face was deathly pale, emphasized more by the bruises about his eyes and nose.

Esther sank to her knees beside Cash. She put the rifle aside and lifted the blanket from her son. She let out a plaintive wail and quickly covered him.

Cash would remember the boy's many wounds until the day he died. Scratches made by fingernails gouged over Danny's chest and groin, but it was the multiple stab wounds in his belly that took the boy's life. And on his purple lips were smudges of strawberry-colored lipstick.

Color drained from Esther's face as she turned to Cash. "You promised neither of us would come to grief!" Tears trailed over her cheeks while her fists pounded his chest. She sobbed, her whole body shaking.

"Danny's death has nothing to do with the election," Cash whispered. "He was killed by a crazy woman." But she didn't seem to hear him, so he let her pummel away, until finally she eased off and her fists opened like bruised flowers to rest in her lap.

Exhausted, she nodded. "I know, I can see that..." Her voice croaking, she added, "I think you should know Dean's last private words to me..."

"Some other time, Esther. You're hurting. Tell me—"

"No," she whispered, persistent. "I'll tell you now. Dean said: 'I know Danny isn't my son, dearest, but I loved him as if he was ...' And he did, he did so very much." Esther lifted a hand to wipe away her tears. "Danny was your son, Cash."

That knife twisted inside him again.

CHAPTER 11

Cold Heart

It seemed as if nobody paid Craig any attention. He gentled his horse round with knee pressure and settled the animal into a canter, away from the dead boy, the wounded mayor and the damnable widow woman.

His bare ass hurt like hell, but he didn't care. Must get away—now!

* * *

Out of the corner of her eye, and even through the tears, Esther detected the movement.

Knowing that Craig had been the man who delivered Danny here, her heart hardened. She grabbed the Winchester.

From her kneeling position, she aimed and fired. She was so numb, she didn't feel the recoil.

She noted with grim satisfaction that a dark shape appeared at the base of Craig's skull. He slumped in the saddle and his bonds prevented him from falling. The horse continued its canter and Craig Bond's body swayed with the motion. His last ride.

* * *

Mayor Nolan laughed. "Good shot, Mrs. Tolliver, but I guess you still lose." He lifted a six-gun from his belt.

But he was too slow, perhaps weakened by his wound. Miles extended his right arm and activated his spring-loaded knife. It struck the mayor's forearm and he dropped the weapon.

Miles looked at Cash and shrugged. "My turn, I reckon. I decided not to kill him. I thought Mrs. T. would appreciate a living opponent."

She shook her head. "I can't go through with the election now. Not after what it has cost me."

Cash got to his feet and helped her up. "Danny wanted you to, Esther. This is your day. Do this for him."

She leaned in against him, silent. He was sure he felt her heart rending apart.

Gently, he led her into the arms of Miles. "Take her back to town," he told Miles. "Help her win that damned election."

Miles nodded.

Her eyes searched his face, an unvoiced question.

"This is something I have to do alone," Cash said.

* * *

He knew where Angelina Nolan had last been—at the entrance to the gully, before the ambush. As she hadn't come through the gully, she must have ridden back along the road. He'd start there.

His heart was cold, his senses at a heightened state by the time he reached the gully.

It only took a few minutes before he identified her horse tracks.

Grimly, he followed the trail. It led toward the fork, where there was a signpost for the Jacobson ranch in one direction and Bear Pines in the other.

Her tracks led to the Jacobson spread.

He couldn't fathom why she'd want to go there, but geed Paint that way.

* * *

Lance Jacobson's face showed surprise as he saw Mrs. Nolan walking in, leading her horse, which had a limp. He stood up from his chair on the porch, a tall powerfully built man in a red-checked shirt and jeans. He waved and welcomed her. "Throw a shoe?" he added.

She nodded and wiped dust from her face. "Yes, not long after I took the fork. I was coming to visit you and decided to carry on as I thought your place is closer than town, anyway."

"I'll get Snark to reshoe the horse. Come and sit a while, 'til it's done."

"Thank you kindly, Lance."

She sat on a chair next to him. On a small table by the chairs was a bottle of whiskey and several tumblers. She slid a tongue over dry lips.

Turning in his chair, Jacobson bawled, "Prentice!"

An elderly man rushed out. He wore an apron and black clothes. "Sir?"

"Take Mrs. Nolan's horse over to Snark and get a new shoe put on, will you?"

"Yes, sir, right away." Nodding fleetingly at Angelina, Prentice rushed down the steps and took the horse away.

Jacobson poured her a drink.

Her hand trembled slightly as she drank it in one gulp. God, she needed that. She held out the glass for another measure, her hand much steadier.

"So, what brings you here, Mrs. Nolan?" he asked, refilling her glass. "Is Brett all right?"

"He's fine," she said, sipping her second drink. "Looking forward to the election results later today, of course."

Jacobson screwed up his face. "Damned election. I've already been to town and voted, of course, but it rankled. The election cost me a good son!"

A chill ran down her spine. "But Jerry's murder had nothing to do with the election."

"Sure it did. If there was no election, that damned marshal wouldn't have been in our town."

She nodded. "Yes, I suppose you're right. In fact, that's what I've come to you about."

"Oh?"

"I fear that the marshal might have slain our good sheriff."

Jacobson swore then added, "Sorry, Mrs. Nolan ..." He clenched his fists. "Hain locked up my boy and those lads, but he said it was only for a few days, 'til the election was over. He promised. Otherwise ..."

"Otherwise?" she prompted, emptying her glass.

"Otherwise, I'd have ridden into Bear Pines and sprung Matt and the others." He refilled her glass. "What happened, how'd the sheriff get killed?"

"He had a disagreement about some point of law, as I understand it." She shrugged. "Sheriff Hain was never going to be fast enough to outdraw that marshal. He was a fool to even try." She was convinced the sheriff and Bond had failed—there'd been too much shooting.

"Brett will sorely miss Hain's support. Today, of all days."

"That's one vote less, certainly." She smiled at him. "So, the sheriff's promise no longer holds, does it?"

"No, I don't suppose it does."

"What are you going to do now, Lance Jacobson?" If she could entice Jacobson to go up against those marshals, then everything could still work out fine.

"I might get the boys together and ..." He paused and then stood up and peered at the ranch entrance. "What the hell?"

Angelina got to her feet and followed his gaze. She felt the blood drain from her face.

Marshal Cash Laramie sat astride his pinto, under the Jacobson shingle. As if he hadn't a care in the world, he smoked a cheroot. He seemed to be waiting.

"What are you going to do now, Lance Jacobson?" she repeated.

CHAPTER 12

A Strange One

Slowly, taking a measured step, Jacobson reached up and clanged the metal triangle that hung from the veranda roof. Usually the call to lunch, it was also employed on rare occasions to raise an alarm.

Cash Laramie didn't make a move.

Barely a minute passed and then six ranch hands emerged from the bunkhouse and hurried over to the porch.

"What's up, boss?" asked the oldest, a big, grizzled man with a bushy brown beard and unkempt hair.

"Seems we've got a killer marshal paying us a visit, Dutch," said Jacobson. "He killed my son Jerry and locked up my Matt and your pals."

Dutch's face darkened and his eyes narrowed. "Maybe this particular marshal needs showing how we do justice out here."

"My thoughts, exactly," Jacobson said.

Angelina sensed the blood coursing through her veins while the warmth of the brandy spread in her gut. She felt her cheeks flush with anticipation. Maybe the marshal's death wouldn't affect the election's outcome, but it would certainly please her. She slid her tongue over her lips.

Jacobson studied the tableau in front of him and folded his arms across his chest. "Before I set my boys on you, Marshal, do you care to tell me what you want here?"

"Are you after killing someone else?" suggested Dutch.

The other hands growled and mumbled.

"I'm here to arrest Mrs. Nolan."

Her heart skipped. She hadn't expected that. "You must be joking!" She laughed and looked at Jacobson.

The rancher eyed her, puzzled. Without taking his eyes off her, Jacobson called, "Why? What's the charge?"

She closed her hand on the Derringer in her skirt pocket. This wasn't happening! A few seconds ago, they were all set to gun down the damned lawman.

"Murder," Cash Laramie said.

The six hands standing around the marshal's horse murmured to each other. She noticed that a couple of the men hesitantly took a few steps back, away from the lawman.

"You must be mistaken, Marshal," Angelina said, gesturing dismissively with her free hand.

"Who was murdered?" Dutch asked.

"A young boy." Cash Laramie's voice grated, rough. He kept his blue eyes on Angelina, unblinking. "Mrs. Tolliver's son, Danny."

She reached out, a hand on Jacobson's arm. "This is absurd, Lance."

"Why would the marshal lie, Mrs. Nolan?" Jacobson asked, removing her hand.

"I'm not going with you, Marshal," she said. "You killed my Jerry—"

"*Your* Jerry?" Jacobson queried, his eyes suddenly cold, narrowed.

She stamped her foot on the boards, quick to change the subject. "Can't you see? He's in league with Mrs. Tolliver. They'd do anything to thwart my husband's chances." She felt blood rise to her face. She was hot, annoyed. Damn Jacobson! "He wants Mrs. Tolliver to win the election by foul means."

Cash Laramie dismounted. He nodded to the hands clustered round him. They backed off, made way for him. He walked slowly, deliberately toward her.

"You talk a lot of hog-swill, Mrs. Nolan," Cash said. "You tortured and then butchered a defenseless young man to satisfy your demented urges."

"Urges?" whispered Dutch to one of his men. "What urges?"

"Dunno, but she doesn't seem too happy about what the marshal's saying," the man said. "Not one bit."

Angelina trembled, her eyes switching from Jacobson to the marshal and then to the men. They all watched her. And she couldn't say anything, couldn't get any words past her tightly compressed lips.

Marshal Cash Laramie climbed the steps in front of her.

His eyes were blue, like cold ice, and they cut into her brain.

She pulled out the Derringer and fired.

* * *

Cash cleared leather with lightning speed and fired almost point blank into her face. Standing slightly below her, his aim had been at an awkward angle. The .45 slug tore away her pert nose and her left eye. She jerked backward, her body's nerves performing a final instruction, pulling the trigger. The .22 Derringer bullet hit the earth at Dutch's feet and he swore.

Angelina Nolan fell back onto the porch boards, two feet away from Jacobson.

Cash turned on the top step, eyed the men. Nobody reached for a weapon.

"Fair, I guess," Jacobson allowed. "At that close range, her gun could've done you real damage, Marshal."

"I couldn't agree more." Cash holstered his Colt. "I'm sorry about your boy, sir. But he wouldn't listen. He drew on me—I had no choice."

Jacobson nodded. "I know, the barkeep said. Jerry was always a mite headstrong. But that day, something got into him, I'm sure. He wouldn't normally behave like that."

"Her words not only condemned her," Cash said "I reckon they explained what got into your Jerry."

Jacobson sighed.

"I'm going back to town now," Cash said. "I'll tell Zeke to free Matt and the others. I think there's been enough bad blood around here for quite a while." He kicked Mrs. Nolan's feet. "And I wouldn't be surprised if a lot of it could be laid at her door."

"She was a strange one, that's a fact. Anyway, that's decent of you, Marshal."

Defaced

Cash rode into town to the sound of firecrackers. A small brass band was playing outside the town hall. The doors were open, the vacant polling booths draped with banners and ribbons. Whistles blew, cheers roared. Guess I missed all the fun, he thought as he reined in outside the sheriff's office. He dismounted, draped the reins over the rail and climbed the steps.

Zeke walked out to meet him. "It's all over, Marshal," he said, beaming.

"I take it Mrs. Tolliver won?"

"She sure did!"

At that moment, the banker, Martin Plampin strolled up. "I always said she'd beat Nolan. My money was on her from the outset."

"Your money, not the bank's?" Cash queried.

Plampin's cheeks wobbled. "Of course, Marshal, of course!"

"Where's Mrs. Tolliver?" Cash asked.

Zeke pointed to the Wordsworth Hotel. "They've laid on a special banquet for her."

Unfastening his reins, Cash turned to Zeke. "You'll need to send Mr. Peel on another errand—out to the Jacobson ranch."

Banker Martin Plampin gasped. "Good God, you haven't killed Lance, have you?"

"No." He pulled out a cheroot, lit it. "And, Zeke, let out Matt and his boys and send them along with the undertaker. I won't press charges."

"Sure thing, Marshal." Zeke hurried toward the undertaker's.

Leading his pinto, Cash walked on to the hotel.

The bunting was dust-covered and hung forlorn from the rooftops of several buildings. A couple of posters for Mayor Nolan had been defaced.

At the hotel, he tied the reins to the hitching rail and patted the pinto. "I won't be long. Then we'll get you some rest and grub." Paint nuzzled his hand.

Feeling weary, he slowly climbed up the steps and entered the hotel foyer. He followed the hubbub of voices and went into the restaurant.

Standing amidst a good number of businessmen and worthies on the stage at the far end of the room, Esther raised her arms and acknowledged the cheers from the floor. Behind her stood the forlorn figure of Brett Nolan, his arm in a sling, his free hand cuffed to the wrist of Burt, the second deputy. Ever vigilant, Miles was by her side.

"Thank you, one and all," Esther said. Her mouth offered a smile, but her eyes were somber. She'd worked hard for this day, and it should have been one of jubilation. Instead, it was heartbreakingly sad.

"I promise to make this town a better place for all of us." Tears flowed down her cheeks. "Somewhere that favors good honest work. I vow on my son's life, Bear Pines will not shelter the dark force of unreason. We will shine like a beacon of goodness."

Miles stepped down and walked over to Cash. "How you feeling?"

"I'll do," Cash said.

"Where's Mrs. Nolan?" Miles asked.

Cash said, "The bitch is dead."

Author Acknowledgments

Thanks to David for asking. And as ever, grateful thanks to Chuck Tyrell for his editing input. (2012)

About the Author

Nik Morton is the author of over 30 books, among them the crime thriller *The Bread of Tears* (reprint of *Pain Wears No Mask*); a romantic thriller set in Tenerife, *An Evil Trade* (reprint of *Blood of the Dragon Trees*); a modern-day vampire and black magic thriller set in Malta, *Chill of the Shadow*. Also, the Tana Standish psychic spy series, *Mission: Prague*, *Mission: Tehran* and *Mission: Khyber* (Manatee Books), plus the westerns *Bullets for a Ballot* and *Coffin for Cash* and a sci-fi book *Continuity Girl* (all from BTAP). He's the editor of *A Fistful of Legends, 21 stories of the Old West*. His writing guide *Write a Western in 30 Days* is useful to writers in all genre fiction. Writing as Ross Morton, Nik has 6 western novels published in the BHW imprint: *Death at Bethesda Falls*, *Last Chance Saloon*, *The $300 Man*, *Blind Justice at Wedlock*, *Old Guns* and *The Magnificent Mendozas*.

He has co-written (with Gordon Faulkner; joint pen-name Morton Faulkner) a fantasy series *Floreskand: Wings*, *Floreskand: King*, *Floreskand: Madurava* and the fourth, *Floreskand: Prophecy*, which was published in November 2021 (all Manatee Books).

He sold his first story in 1971 and has had over 100 short stories published—some winning awards—in various genres, among them action, adventure, romance, ghost, horror, sci-fi, western and crime. They are collected in 6 volumes (comprising 121 stories): *Gifts from a Dead Race*, *Nourish a Blind Life*, *Visitors*, *Codename Gaby*, *I Celebrate Myself* and *Leon Cazador, P.I.*

For over forty years, he has edited periodicals and contributed hundreds of articles, book and film reviews. He has chaired several writers' circles and run writing and screenplay workshops. Since 1995, he has edited books and, for the period 2003–2007, he was sub-editor of the monthly colour magazine, *Portsmouth Post*, and for 2011–2013 he was Editor in Chief of a US publisher but stepped down to pursue his many writing projects.

He lived in Spain with his wife Jennifer for fifteen years, but they have now moved back to UK, residing in Northumberland. Their daughter, son-in-law, grandson and granddaughter live nearby.